STOLEN RELICS

MACKENZIE GREY: TRIALS #4

KARINA ESPINOSA

ISBN-13: 9798646903298
ASIN: B088SC4HQ7

For my readers.
This one is for you.

1

It was scorching hot and the A/C unit in the car was busted. The windows were down and muggy air blew inside, not cooling us down one bit. My tank top clung to my sticky skin, and I was pretty sure if I wrung it out, gallons of water would seep out. I didn't know how much more of this I could take. It was bad enough my body already ran at a high temperature, but this was just torture.

"All right, Grey, what kind of hero do you want?" Michaels asked as he parked the unmarked police car near a fire hydrant in front of a bodega. He unbuckled his seat belt and turned off the engine.

"Pastrami. The works." I wiped more sweat off my neck. "And water. Ice cold water."

"You got it." He got out of the car and strode into the bodega to buy us lunch.

I stayed in the car to stave off the heat and listen to the police scanner for any incidents in the area. We were on patrol and things had been relatively quiet since my return. I'd been back with the SIU for three weeks, and besides a few minor infractions, we hadn't had any major cases. It was actually quite dull. Normally, I'd be somewhat peeved and in need of some action, but after everything I'd gone through recently, a little quiet was just what I needed. I was just happy to be back on the team. After getting suspended, it was no easy feat getting back in the SIU. I was embarrassed to admit it required Alexander's help. He made a few calls, issued a few threats, and I was back on the force. Not that the threats I made didn't work, but his held a little more weight, being the King of the Lycans and all.

Now I was keeping a low profile. Someone in the Supernatural Investigative Unit didn't want me there, for reasons I didn't know. I had a couple options: I could dig into it, or let it go and go about my business. Currently, I was going with option two, but that could change at the drop of a hat. Right now just wasn't the time to be meddling in things I should probably stay away from. I had bigger problems to worry about. Like my brother.

Oliver Grey gave up his career, his life, everything to move back home to be near me. If only I knew what that actually meant. Ollie didn't want to be close to me simply because we were family; he wanted to be close to me so he could investigate. Ever since the night with Enzo and his wolf sighting, he's been building a case. I realize now I should have listened to Cassidy when he warned me.

I'd always thought of my brother as a reasonable person, someone who wouldn't believe in the supernatural world, but I supposed when you saw things, you felt compelled to see it again to convince yourself you didn't imagine it. And that was what he did. He followed me until he saw what he wanted to see. Unfortunately, he got bit in the process. I bit him, and now he'll be just like me. I hated myself for what I did to him and what he'll go through. He deserved better. To be far away from it all.

Now the full moon was coming up and he would shift for the first time. It would be the most painful experience of his life. He wasn't ready. Neither was I.

The car door opened, and Michaels hopped in with a brown paper bag and two ice cold bottles of water balanced in his arms.

"Oh my God, gimme!" I grabbed one of the bottles and put it behind my neck. The shock of cold condensation on my over-heated skin made a chill run through my body.

"You're welcome," Michaels snorted. "Ah shit, I forgot to get napkins." He dug through the brown paper bag, looking for the missing items.

"I'll get them if you want—" I said when the police scanner crackled.

"10-31, The Third Eye," the dispatcher reported through the scanner. "Any available units?"

"That's a burglary in progress," Michaels said as he wrapped up the brown paper bag with our sandwiches and tossed it in the back seat. He turned on the car and I grabbed the receiver and responded to dispatch, letting them know we were on the way.

The Third Eye was one of the biggest supernatural bars in New York, and well known for corruption. There were rumors that the owner was linked with someone high up in the SIU, but no one had been able to find any concrete evidence. I'd been there a few times, most recently when I was on the run and trying to get information on the vampires. If the place was getting robbed during the day, it couldn't be good.

Michaels turned on the sirens and we sped through the city

streets. We weren't far from the bar – just a few blocks away – but with Manhattan traffic, it would feel like hours.

When we finally pulled up in front of the bar, we hopped out, reaching for our guns.

"I'll take the front, you take the back," I whispered to Michaels and he nodded, running to the back exit of the bar. I gave him a few seconds to get in place before I opened the front door and peered inside.

The inside looked the same as it did the last time I was there. The bar was on the left, the walls were lined with plastic-uphol-stered booths, and the center of the room was scattered with a hodgepodge of mismatched tables and stools. At night it was dim and mysterious, but since it was daytime, the daylight filtered in and I could see how dated the bar was. Paint was chipped and faded. The wood panels of the bar were old. But none of that was more fascinating than what was unfolding in the center of the room. A man was on his knees and another person in a ski mask was hovering over him, a black duffle bag slung over his shoulders and his hand outstretched. A yellowish, white glow fizzled from his fingertips as if threatening to shoot at the man on his knees.

"SIU! Put your hands up!" I shouted as I aimed my gun at the threat before me. He didn't flinch or spare me a glance. "Put out your magic and turn around!"

The magic disappeared in a blink and the person in the ski mask turned around to face me. Just when I thought they'd surrender, they began to shudder, almost vibrating in place at a speed beyond supernatural, then the person spilt into two people, then three. Within seconds, I was facing three of the same person. At least I thought it was the same person.

Before I could register their next move, a blast of magic hit me square in the chest. They threw it so fast, it was as if I'd blinked and it happened. I was thrown back against the opposite wall with a loud thud.

The blast took me by surprise since I had the Celtic triquetra, which looked like a three-cornered infinity knot within a circle, tattooed on my hip that was supposed to protect me from malicious magic. However, it didn't protect me from the *force* of it, just the *intent*.

The rear exit doors burst open and Michaels stormed in firing his gun, but the bullets ricocheted as harmlessly as if the multiples wore bulletproof vests. It did nothing to them. Two of them stayed behind, flinging arcs of magic at Michaels, while the third strode confidently out the front door.

I scrambled to my feet, shaking my head and clearing it from the haze it was in and ran outside. The heat smacked me in the face like a living thing, and it took a minute for my eyes to adjust to the beaming sun that pounded down. When I made it to the sidewalk, there was no sign of the robber. Just dozens of New Yorkers walking the streets where he could have easily gotten lost in a crowd.

I ran back inside the bar only to find Michaels helping the man on his knees up to his feet.

"Where did the other two go?" I called out from across the room as I holstered my gun.

Michaels ran a hand through his hair. "They disappeared. Like, poofed out of existence."

They appeared to be clones, but that couldn't be. There was no way. This was way too sci-fi for me.

"Hello, I'm Detective Grey and this is my partner Detective Michaels. Can you tell us your name?" I asked the man before us.

"Maximos Limogiannis. I'm the owner of The Third Eye." The man gripped the back of a chair tightly, his nostrils flaring. He didn't offer a hand to shake or even a friendly smile. Actually, he looked kind of pissed that we were there. He had shiny, ebony hair that was slicked back with gel and wore pressed slacks, a button-up, and suspenders. Very old-fashioned. Maybe a little mobster looking.

"Ah, it's nice to finally meet the man behind the curtain," I offered with a sardonic smile. "So, tell us Maximos ... was this a deal gone bad?"

"That's really none of the SIU's business."

"Are you serious?" Michaels scoffed and jerked his thumb at the front door. "You were about to get magically barbecued before we showed up. A thank you wouldn't hurt, especially when Grey took the hit for you," he jeered with his thick New York accent.

I touched my chest, rubbed at it and winced. Yeah, that still stung. Whatever that person cooked up was powerful.

"I never called for the SIU, and I definitely don't need them sticking their noses in my business. I won't be filing a report, so you both can leave." Maximos waved us both toward the door imperiously.

I arched a brow. "Unluckily for you, I was hurt, so I *will* be filing a report and following up on what happened here," I said with a large smile on my face. He was hiding something, and I was determined to find out what it was.

"So, what was it that was stolen?" Michaels asked as he pulled out his notepad.

"Nothing."

"Don't lie to us," I tsked and wagged a finger.

Maximos glowered. "I can have your job like this." He snapped his fingers.

I chuckled. "No you can't, but I'd love to see you try."

He pulled out his cellphone and held it up. "One phone call and your job is gone."

"Grey," Michaels muttered, placing a hand on my arm to hold me back, but I refused to back down.

I nodded to Maximos. "Go on. Make your phone call. I'd love to hear this conversation."

Michaels leaned into me and whispered in my ear, "There's confidence, and then there's arrogance. You're towing the line."

"I know what I'm doing," I murmured and cleared my throat. "Make sure you get my name right. Mackenzie Grey MacCoinnich. Please send my regards."

I clasped my hands in front of me and waited as I watched Maximos' expression go from self-assured, to pensive, to oh-shit-what-did-she-say, to fuck. I should have recorded the myriad of emotions.

Maximos steeled himself, straightening and locking his jaw. "You're the Curse Breaker." It was more of a statement than a question.

"I guess Freedom Princess went out of style," I muttered.

"I'm not afraid of you," he declared, almost trying to convince himself instead of me.

I shook my head and rolled my eyes. "I'm not trying to scare you, you fool. I'm trying to help you. You're obviously in some sort of trouble, but threatening me is not the solution. I'm not afraid of you either, so the feeling is mutual. Now will you let us do our job, or will we have to do this the hard way?"

Michaels reached for the iron handcuffs on his hips and Maximos' eyes followed his movements. The message was clear. Either he told us what we wanted to know, or we took him in using very uncomfortable methods. I didn't know what species he was, but iron usually did the trick unless he was Lycan, which I doubted. No wolf would be this much of a sleaze.

The bar owner held up his hands and relented. "Fine, no need to get rough." He backed up to one of the stools by the bar and sat down, letting out a breath. "That was a Gemini that came in here. They're a nasty species and extremely rare. Usually they're hired as hit men, so obviously one was hired to ransack my safe."

"Obviously." I rolled my eyes. "Now what's in your safe that would make someone put a hit out on you?"

Maximos gritted his teeth and looked away. "Besides a ton of money and gold?"

"Yes, smart ass," Michaels chimed in.

"I also collect rare artifacts. One of them is the Draupnir."

"What?" I frowned as I looked between him and Michaels.

Michaels laughed. "You're joking, right? That's impossible."

Maximos smirked. "I do not lie, detective. See for yourself." He waved toward the back office.

I slapped Michaels in the arm and gave him a 'what the fuck' face. "Care to fill me in?"

He sighed. "I only know what he's talking about because I read comic books as a kid, so I know this is all bullshit."

"I don't care; what is it?" I said.

"Draupnir is a golden ring possessed by Odin the Norse God.

It's supposed to duplicate like, eight rings or some shit. In other words, it makes you super rich. It was made by the same people that made Thor's hammer."

I stared at my partner to make sure he was being for real and wasn't joking. When he didn't elaborate further, I realized he was being serious. "That's it, cuff him." I pointed to Maximos.

Michaels didn't hesitate to pull out the iron handcuffs and grab Maximos by the arm, hauling him out of his seat and slamming him against the bar, face forward.

"I'm telling you guys the truth! This is real!"

I snorted. "Yeah, and the tooth fairy also gave me a dollar when I was five. Get real."

Michaels subdued him, and once the iron cuffs were secured, Maximos lost all his strength, making it easy to drag him to our unmarked police car out front.

What a day.

2

We made it back to the station where Finn and Cassidy were already at their desks in the squad room waiting for us. Michaels took Maximos to an interrogation room to sweat it out while I plopped down at my desk with my uneaten hero and empty water bottle. The heat was killer outside and the air conditioner in the building was a welcomed reprieve.

"How is it out there?" Cassidy Chang asked as he threw a balled-up piece of paper at me. It was funny looking at his hulking figure in that small seat.

"It's hot as shit," I said breathlessly. "Other than that, guess who we brought in?" I grinned mischievously.

He raised a thick brow.

"Maximos Limogiannis. The owner of The Third Eye."

"You didn't," Finn marveled as he walked over and perched on the corner of my desk and started fiddling with my pens, his pitch-black hair flopping over his forehead.

"*We* did." I snatched my good pen from him before he stole it.

"We got called in for a 10-31, but then the suspect got away and Maximos didn't want to cooperate. He knows more than he's telling."

Cassidy frowned. "Let me get this straight. He almost got robbed, but he doesn't want to catch the guy who did it?"

I threw his paper ball back at him. "Why does the robber have to be a guy? It could have been a woman."

"Was it though?" Finn smirked.

I rolled my eyes. "Fine, it was a dude. It was something called a Gemini. Ever heard of them?"

Finn grimaced. "They're nasty. You were definitely outmatched. Literally. Whoever is after Maximos really must hate him."

"Well, whatever it is, he'll eventually crack," Cassidy offered smugly as he leaned back in his chair.

The guys started telling me about their patrol in the subways while I finished eating my late lunch. As I listened, I realized how much I'd missed this comradery. Though it had only been a few weeks, it felt like a lifetime. I could only imagine how I would feel when I had to give this up for good. It just meant I needed to soak up every moment until then.

"He lawyered up," Michaels said disgustedly as he stomped back into the squad room. "Bastard."

I shrugged. "We don't have much to hold him anyway. It's all good."

Michaels sat at his desk across from mine and started to eat his lunch. "He was going on with some really crazy stories. That guy has some screws loose."

I nodded. "We'll talk to Briggs and open an investigation, maybe stake out The Third Eye."

My phone buzzed in my pocket and I pulled it out while the guys talked, cringing when I saw the name that popped up on the screen. Alexander. I'd been avoiding his calls lately. I hit decline and shot him a text, informing him I'd call him tonight, which I would actually have to do. He was the last person I should be avoiding, but after what happened to Ollie, I didn't know how to tell him what I did. I knew he'd be disappointed in me. After everything I'd already done to him, I just couldn't handle it. Alexander was better off finding someone else to take over the throne. I was a complete fuck up.

"Hey, you okay?" Cassidy said as he squatted beside me.

I snapped out of my daze and set my phone down on my desk, plastering on a fake smile. "Yeah, of course."

He tilted his head. "Grey, you're a horrible liar."

I pushed him and laughed. "I'm fine, I swear." No one besides the Brooklyn Pack knew what I'd done. Even though I trusted Cas, I couldn't tell him. Biting humans was taboo, and I wasn't ready for him to look at me differently.

The door to Lieutenant Owens Briggs's office flew open, making our gazes snap in that direction as his short, bulky form stomped out of his office. He was red faced, his bald head shining under the fluorescent lights, and you could practically see steam spewing out of his ears.

"Who the hell brought in Maximos Limogiannis?" he yelled in the squad room.

Cas and I looked at one another and then I looked at Michaels, who was mid-bite with his sandwich, eyes wide.

I stood from my desk uneasily and took a couple steps toward Briggs. "I did. What's the problem?"

Michaels swallowed quickly and hurried to my side. "*We* did. He was obstructing an investigation."

Briggs growled loudly and reached for his head as if he had hair he wanted to pull. I had to smash my lips tightly to hold in my laughter.

"Cut him loose! Now!" he shouted so loud you could hear him from New Jersey.

I stepped forward. "But why? We did everything right—"

"I said, cut him loose! Right this second! No buts!" he screamed before storming back into his office and slamming the door, making the glass windows rattle. We all jumped from the force.

My gaze snapped back to my team and we just looked at each other, knowing exactly what had happened. There were rumors of corruption throughout the higher-ups of the SIU, rumors of them giving special treatment to The Third Eye, letting them get away with a laundry list of crimes. This was proof.

Finn cleared his throat. "Don't worry, I'll let him go." Without another word, he left the squad room and headed to the interrogation room while we were left to look at one another.

"This is bullshit," Michaels breathed, breaking the silence.

"What are you thinking, Grey?" Cas looked at me warily.

I didn't answer. I turned back to Briggs's office and watched it from behind the blinds. I'd hoped to stay under the radar, but after today, maybe I should make a little noise.

AFTER WHAT FELT like the longest day ever, I finally took the train out of Manhattan and back to Brooklyn. This was the only thing I didn't like about my new living arrangement—the commute to work. It meant I had to wake up earlier and come home later, but I was getting used to it, I guess. I'd only been doing it for a couple weeks since I got back on the team, but it was getting easier.

I passed the Compound and went around the corner to our brownstone where I unlocked the door, locked it behind me, and dropped my bag by the door. The smell of garlic was heavy in the air and I followed my nose to the kitchen. Standing in front of the stove was my brother, Oliver Grey, wearing an apron over his clothes and stirring a pot of pasta.

"Hey," I said, trying not to startle him since his back was to me.

He looked over his shoulder at me and smiled. "Hey, sis. How was work?"

I blew out a breath. "Rough day. Not really a pleasant topic. How was your day?"

After stirring the pasta, he put the wooden spoon to the side and turned to fully face me. "I spent the day with Sebastian. He's upstairs taking a shower. We went for a run in the park."

"A run?" I raised a brow.

He nodded. "It seems I have a lot of excess energy to prepare for my first shift."

"Are you taking the tonic Waldo gave you?" I asked, knowing it hurt him, but that he needed it to make the shift less painful.

Ollie grimaced. "Yeah, I take it first thing in the morning to get it out of the way."

I turned away from him then, because looking at Ollie broke my heart. Recently, the more I stared at him, the more I saw our differences. The only similarity we ever really had was our eyes and maybe our hair color, but our features were so different. I never really noticed before, but maybe it was because I didn't want to. Even so, he was still my brother and I loved him no matter what our DNA said. Which was why the knowledge of what I did to him hurt so much. From the outside, it seemed like he was fine, but I knew him better than that. He always bottled everything up, but I was pretty sure he was freaking out on the inside.

"Have you spoken to Mom and Dad?" I asked as I went to go wash my hands at the kitchen sink.

"Yeah, they want us to come home soon. I was able to get us out of dinner this weekend for obvious reasons." Left unspoken was, *Because I'll be shifting for the first time.* "But the following weekend, we might have to take a trip to Cold Springs."

I nodded. "I can get the time off work, that's not a problem."

Ollie gently took hold of my arm and turned me around to face him. "Kenz, I'm not mad at you, so don't be mad at yourself."

I couldn't look him in the eyes, so I dropped my gaze to the floor. He tugged on my arm.

"Kenzie, stop it. This isn't ideal, but it happened. Let's make the best of it."

My gaze snapped to his. "The *best* of it? There's nothing good about this!"

"You mean to tell me you're unhappy with the way you are?" he asked.

I scoffed. "I didn't say that. I just—this life is dangerous. I didn't want this for you." What I really wanted to say was that anyone connected to me was in danger, but I didn't want to scare him or make him even more protective of me than he already was. If – or more like *when* – people found out he was my brother, they could use him against me as leverage. I would do anything

15

for him, which put me in a very difficult situation and him in a dangerous one.

He kissed me on the forehead. "I know danger, Kenz. Don't worry about me." Ollie let me go and went back to cooking dinner.

I left the kitchen, not bothering to argue, and dragged myself upstairs to my bedroom. The shower wasn't running anymore, so I knew Bash would be coming out soon.

I threw myself on our bed, crossed my feet at the ankles, and pulled my cell phone out of my pocket, scrolling through my messages. There was one from Alexander that he sent thirty minutes ago reminding me to call him. I sighed, realizing there was no point holding out any longer.

Pressing his name, I hit the call button and the phone started to ring. After two rings, he answered.

"Mackenzie!" he announced in his thick Scottish brogue. "Why have ye nae answered my calls? Is everything okay?"

In that moment, Bash walked out of the bathroom with a towel wrapped around his waist. He gave me a questioning look.

"Everything is fine, Alexander," I responded pointedly. Bash nodded in understanding and continued to walk around our bedroom to his dresser to pull out clean clothes.

"It's been weeks since ye called me, darling. Ye know I worry."

I gnawed on my bottom lip, wondering how I would bring Ollie up in conversation. "I know, Alexander. I'm sorry, I've just been dealing with a lot lately—"

"Does this have to do with yer job, Mackenzie? I called them—"

"No! It doesn't, you did great. I got my job back and I've been working. It has nothing to do with that."

I hated using the MacCoinnich name to get special privileges, but Briggs had insisted I use it while I was on administrative leave from the Supernatural Investigative Unit. Alexander called the higher-ups at the SIU and pulled some strings for me to get my job back. Even though he didn't want me working, especially in this profession, he knew it made me happy and was willing to threaten them to make it happen.

"That's good, darling. I'm glad everything worked out." He sounded so genuine. Alexander would lasso the moon and bring it down for me if I really wanted it. It was why I hated disappointing him.

"Alexander," I whispered into the phone, "I'm so sorry." I closed my eyes as if he were right in front of me and could see the shame on my face.

"What's wrong?" he said softly.

"I don't deserve the crown. Is there anyone else who can inherit it? A cousin, maybe? Please," I begged.

There was silence on the phone line, and for a moment, I thought I'd lost the connection. I opened my eyes and Bash had dressed himself in a pair of sweats and a t-shirt and was sitting at the foot of the bed. His piercing blue eyes were on me, but his neutral expression meant I couldn't gauge his thoughts.

"Mackenzie," Alexander said carefully, "if yer nae anointed Queen, the MacCoinnich family loses the crown. I know yer nae ready now, but what has ye so scared?"

I brought my knees to my chest and rested my forehead on them. "I did something you're not going to like, Alexander. It was a mistake. I did it to save a life, it was unavoidable, but it happened. I didn't even realize what happened until afterward. It wasn't my intention."

"What did ye do, Mackenzie?" he said sternly.

"I bit my brother."

"Bloody hell," he breathed into the phone. Before I could respond, Bash snatched my cell phone from me.

"Your Highness, it's Sebastian Steel," he said, turning his back to me as he started to pace the room. "Please let me explain to you what happened."

I could listen in on their conversation, but I didn't really want to. Alexander wasn't mad. He didn't get mad at me, but he was disappointed, and that was infinitely worse. I almost wished he would scream at me and get it over with. I was a walking, talking, PR nightmare.

Bash went into great detail on what had happened with Bobby Wu. I didn't expect him to tell him that part, so it caught me off guard. But he told him how the warlock and I were bound together, and how Bobby kidnapped Ollie because he'd been following me around. How Bobby compelled Ollie to jump out of a tree to try and force me to shift back to human so he could control me, and then how while in wolf form, I latched onto him to stop him from falling, which meant I bit him. Honestly, I didn't mean to, I just didn't want my brother to fall.

Bash and Alexander went back and forth for about fifteen minutes before Bash passed me the phone again.

"Hello?" I answered tremulously.

"Mackenzie," Alexander voiced so calmly, I couldn't get a read on his mood, "I'm flying out to America this weekend. Sebastian said ye can have me in yer home."

My eyes widened and I looked at Bash. "Alexander, you don't have to come here—"

"It's time for a visit. I'll see ye soon, darling," he said more softly. The call ended and I looked down at my phone, dumb-founded.

"Bash, how could you?" I peered up at him. He stood at the end of the bed with his arms crossed over his chest.

"He needed to know what's been going on with you, Mackenzie. He never would've understood how Oliver got bit any other way."

"That wasn't your decision to make!" I yelled, my eyes wild. I took a deep breath, trying to control myself and settle down. "I would have told him," I added more calmly.

Bash tilted his head. "No, you wouldn't have, but that's okay. I think it's good that he'll be here. You need to spend more time with him."

I smashed my lips together, trying to hold in the outburst that surely wanted to explode from me. Yeah, I wanted to spend time with Alexander, but under better circumstances. It felt almost like he was being forced to come discipline me.

"I'm not a child, Sebastian. Stop treating me like one." I stood from the bed and started to make my way out of the bedroom.

"Hey, wait a second." He grabbed my hand as I started to stomp past. "That wasn't my intention, Mackenzie. I'm sorry."

I peered up at Bash and his features softened. "Let's just go eat dinner," I mumbled and walked out of the room.

He didn't immediately follow me, and I was glad. I didn't want him hovering like a helicopter parent. One of the personality quirks that Bash still worked on was his protectiveness and how far he took it. I knew he meant well, which was why I tried not to blow up every time he did it, but it wasn't easy. Especially when it involved Alexander. That was *my* business, and I should be responsible for it, not him.

3
_____

The week went by fast, and Michaels and I were lucky to only get a verbal warning at work after arresting Maximos. If it wasn't because I had family obligations, I'd be all over that and trying to figure out what the hell happened. But that would have to wait.

Ollie and I sat in the backseat of Bash's SUV as we entered Cadwell Estate and drove down the three-mile, winding road that led to the house. My brother's face was plastered to the window as he watched the wolves that raced beside the car as they escorted us to the house. I reached over to his car door and lowered his window so he could breathe in the fresh air of the woods. We were in over a hundred acres of terrain. It had rained recently, and I took a deep breath and smelled it in the air.

"This is where I'm shifting?" Ollie turned to look at me with expectant eyes.

I grimaced. "Not exactly."

Since this was Ollie's first shift and it wasn't natural, it had to be contained. He wouldn't be shifting with the rest of the Pack out on the land, he would be in the cage—the silver cage —heavily sedated and weakened so he wouldn't feel the pain as much. The tonics Waldo made before he left were intended to prepare his body for this, but even so the pain would be ten times worse than when a wolf was moon bound. During this shift, he would feel excruciating pain as his bones rearranged to accept their new form, since he wasn't born to shift into a wolf.

I hated that he was forced to go through all this pain, but I vowed to be with him through it all. I wasn't shifting tonight so I could stay with Ollie. If not, he would be alone, and I didn't want that for him. He didn't deserve that.

We pulled up to the house and there were already people milling around, half-dressed and getting ready to start bonfires and barbecues. Ollie and I exited the car from our respective sides and met at the back of the SUV. Bash and Jackson got out and headed inside to talk to Charles and get the basement ready.

"I'm nervous," Ollie admitted as he peered around the woods, taking it all in.

I craned my neck and stared at him. "I'd be surprised if you weren't." I reached for his hand. "I'll be with you every step of the way. We'll do this together."

He looked down at me. "Don't you have to shift, too?"

I shook my head. "Not tonight. I will tomorrow. Tonight, it's all about you and getting you through the night."

He gulped and his hands started to get clammy. "Kenz, if I don't make it—"

"Don't say that! You're going to be fine. You survived the Middle East; you can do anything."

He snorted. "This is on a whole other level, Kenzie, and you know it."

There was a ponderous silence between us, and I couldn't respond to him because he was right. This was a different beast. But I had all the faith in the world that he'd make it out. He had to. I couldn't imagine a world without Ollie in it.

"Mackenzie!" Bash called from the top step of the estate.

I turned to him. "Yeah?"

"It's ready."

I swallowed loudly and squeezed Ollie's hand. The sun wasn't due to set for a few more hours, but we needed to prepare.

As Bash led us inside the mansion, I looked at the surroundings with fresh eyes. It still felt like walking into a museum with priceless objects scattered around and expensive art on the walls. We followed Bash down an Oriental rug-blanketed hallway that brought back dark memories of the night the Lunas were massacred and I found V's lifeless body lying halfway in the corridor. I shut my eyes to block the images of blood-splattered walls and floors and continued down the hall until we reached the door at the end that led to the basement where I was once held.

We walked down the stairs and my eyes adjusted to the dimly lit room. At the far end of the room by the wall was the silver cage. It was large enough for a wolf to roam around in wolf form, but definitely not run.

In the middle of the room was a table with a couple bottles of liquid I recognized as the tonics Waldo had given Ollie when he was first bitten. It was what my brother had been taking every day since to get his body accustomed to the change, but I knew it would still be extremely painful.

I could still hear his screams from that day.

Bash looked at his watch. "In an hour or so, give him the first tonic, but make sure he's in the cage already. Be careful, Mackenzie. You'll feel the effects of the cage as well."

"I understand. This isn't my first time down here."

His brows furrowed. "Even so, be careful. Once Oliver begins to shift, he'll be volatile. He could hurt you unintentionally. It's why this part is meant to be done alone."

I shook my head. "I'm not leaving him."

"Kenz, you don't have to stay—" Ollie started, but I cut him off.

"I'm staying. End of discussion." I held up my hands to shut everyone up. "I know what to do, Bash."

He nodded and came over to me, placing a soft kiss on my forehead. "I'll see you in the morning."

Bash left and it was just me and my brother—and a silver cage.

The first hour dragged on as we waited for the inevitable, but when the time came, Ollie stripped down to his boxers and stepped inside the cage. I could see the bite mark I gave him on his shoulder and knew he would carry that mark for the rest of his life as a reminder of what he was.

When he was ready, I grabbed the tonic bottles and joined him inside the cage. I felt the effects of the silver immediately and stumbled, wavering on my feet as I settled the bottles and lined them up by the bars so we had easy access to them. I took one and met Ollie in the center of the cage.

I handed it over to him. "Bottoms up."

He winced and took it from me, putting the glass to his lips. Hesitating for just a moment, he threw it back and choked on the bitter liquid, almost spitting it out before swallowing it all down.

He fell to the ground on all fours, dry heaving and coughing, spittle flying from his mouth.

I dropped to the ground with him and placed a hand on his back, rubbing circles. "It's okay, Ollie. Just breathe."

He screamed as his whole body shook, the tonic taking hold. I could only watch in horror. There was nothing I could do to lessen the pain. We sat on the floor for about thirty minutes until the pain began to dull, and by the end, he was in the fetal position, shivering as if the room was freezing. I draped my body over his, hoping to warm him up and stop the shakes.

"Is it almost time?" Ollie croaked beneath me.

I typically didn't wear a watch, but I did tonight since I knew that down here, we wouldn't be able to feel the moon.

"You should feel your first bone break very soon. I'll get the next tonic ready." I started to get up, but he latched onto my forearm.

"D-don't leave me," he stuttered as a shiver wracked his body.

I looked over at the bottles lined up by the cage bars and looked down at my brother, whom I'd never seen so vulnerable before.

"AH!" he screamed and arched his back. Even without my sensitive hearing, I could have heard the sound of bones cracking. It was his spine. He squeezed my forearm so tightly, I thought I would lose circulation. His body contorted in ways that weren't humanly possible.

"It's going to be okay, Ollie," I whispered over his screams. "Breathe through the pain." I tried to hold on to him, but he was moving so much, his arm snapping, his legs kicking and distorting, that eventually I had to let him go so he could shift freely.

His screams were unnatural. Though Ollie's eyes were

squeezed firmly shut, tears poured out and streamed down his cheeks. Sweat glistened all over his body as he exerted an enormous amount of energy. He was gritting his teeth so hard I thought they would crack.

I didn't realize I was crying until I licked my lips and tasted the salt. I ran, stumbling from the effects of silver, over to the bars of the cage and grabbed one of the tonics. Bringing it to Ollie, I gripped his cheeks and squeezed his mouth open. I poured the liquid down his throat and he almost choked on it, but it went down. Within seconds, his body relaxed a bit and I threw the empty bottle across the room.

I held on to my brother as his body paused in the transformation cycle. He'd blacked out from the pain. He was completely disfigured, and I couldn't stop the sobs that wracked my body. I stroked his damp hair away from his face and checked to make sure he was still breathing.

After almost an hour, the screaming commenced again. It continued for hours, but it wasn't until midnight that I started to see the wolf. His human legs formed into hind legs, and his face now fit a snout. By one in the morning, he was in full wolf form.

He was beautiful, his coat a dark, glossy brown with silver highlights, and his eyes a golden shade of bright yellow.

He lay on the concrete floor, exhausted and breathing heavily for several minutes. I gave him his space and didn't approach him. After a while, he stood and started to scan the area. He was wobbly, the silver of the cage making him weak, but when those yellow eyes landed on me, he growled. I dropped to one knee and bowed my head, giving him a submissive pose and extending a hand for him to sniff. Tentatively, he approached me, taking a whiff of my hand and prowling closer to my face. His canines were white and sharp, and he was snarling.

"Ollie, it's me," I whispered. "You're still in there. Don't let the wolf take over. Take control."

He huffed and the air blew my hair back, but I didn't dare lift my head just yet. After a couple of tense minutes, I jerked back in surprise as he licked my face.

I lifted my head and laughed. "Is this your version of a wet willie?" I joked, and he did it again. I smiled brightly and went to rub him behind the ear and down his coat. "Good job, Ollie. You did it. After this, I promise I'll never let you get hurt again."

Ollie backed away from me and started to pace the cage, and I knew he was itching to get out of there. We were both weak and tired from the silver, but we were stuck there for the night. Tomorrow would be different.

"How did he do?" Jackson asked as we sat around a dying fire in the woods. After leaving Ollie in the basement to sleep and get some rest, I went searching for Bash. Instead I found Jackson in human form, sitting on a log by a fire. It was odd because the temperature was already sweltering, and the fire only amplified the heat.

"He did great," I beamed. "The first couple hours were rough. I didn't realize how long it would last, but he finally broke through around one in the morning. And when he did, it was amazing."

"Did he recognize you?"

I shook my head. "Not initially, but I told you, Ollie is strong.

He was able to get control of his wolf." I pushed Jackson playfully. "He had yellow eyes, though. I thought he might have—"

"I know what you thought, Kenz." Jackson smiled. "But only MacCoinnichs have silver eyes. No matter what."

I knew that. Obviously, I did. It had been drilled into me since I found out about my lineage. I just hoped that by some miracle ... Well, I didn't know what I hoped for.

"I heard your pops is coming to town," Jackson said, kicking some dirt into the fire to let it die.

"News sure travels fast," I snorted. "Did Bash tell you?"

"He told my dad and I overheard."

Of course he told Charles that the King was coming. Charles Cadwell was such a suck-up. Our relationship still wasn't anything to write home about. The guy hated my guts and continued to blame me for Jonah's death. Not like I didn't carry enough guilt already.

"Alexander will be here Monday. He was going to come for the weekend, but I told him about Ollie shifting and that I wanted privacy." I sighed. "Bash told him everything."

Jackson's head snapped toward me. "Like, *every*thing?"

"Yup. He's pretty much coming here to reprimand me."

He twisted his mouth. "Do you know that for sure?"

"No." I rolled my eyes. "But that's what it feels like."

"You're so dramatic, Kenzie. Alexander worries and cares about you a lot, and he's been itching to come out here for a long time. This was probably just the perfect opportunity," Jackson said, like the reasonable adult he was. I, on the other hand, was irrational.

I shrugged. "I just feel like a little kid. I'm trying to be more responsible, but everyone still handles me."

Jackson snorted. "I don't know what universe you live in, where you think someone is able to handle *you*."

I punched him in the arm. "I'm being serious, jackass."

"I am too. You've never let anyone control you. It's what started the whole rebellion. Why are you getting it through that thick skull that someone is?" I looked away and didn't answer him. Instead, I stared at my sneaker-clad feet as if the answer was there. "Just because you've simmered down, doesn't mean you've lost your touch, Kenz."

"But don't you miss it when I used to—"

"No," Jackson cut me off. "You were a nightmare."

I gasped in mock horror, then we both burst out laughing. We hung out in the woods for a while until we realized no one was coming to look for us. We made our way back to the estate and found Bash and Charles in front of the house.

"There you are!" Bash said as we walked out of the tree line. "I expected to find you in the basement."

"I thought I'd let Ollie get some sleep."

Charles Cadwell, the Alpha of the Northeast region of North America, stood in a pair of jeans and a tucked-in polo shirt. His chestnut hair was combed back in waves and his eyes were the same as Jackson's, a burnished milk chocolate. He stood stonily beside Bash, eyeing me with such hatred and disdain it practically radiated from his pores.

"Mackenzie," Charles said. "A pleasure, as always."

"Charles, how are you?" I tried to plaster a genuine smile on my face, but it felt stiff.

He ignored me and got right to the point. "I hear your father is coming for a visit, after another disappointment of yours. Such a shame *this* is what the Lycans' future holds."

Bash stiffened and glared in his direction but didn't say anything. He couldn't. That was his Alpha and he was already on thin ice. I didn't blame him.

Jackson, however, wasn't under the same allegiance. "Father!"

I placed a hand on Jackson's arm to stop him. "It's no secret I make mistakes."

"Of course they're not secrets. You're so loud, the whole community is aware of your every move!" Charles spat disgustedly.

I gave him a tight smile. "Yes, it does make me well known. Liked by some, feared by others. Almost like how a ruler *should* be, wouldn't you say?" I tilted my head, but he only glared at me. "The important thing is that I learn from my mistakes. That's what will make me a good leader. And at the end of the day you're stuck with me, so quit your whining."

As Charles marched toward me Jackson moved to stand in front of me, but I pushed him aside. I could face off with his father. The last person on the planet I feared was Charles Cadwell.

He got in my face and I smirked, only pissing him off further. "You will not survive in our world, and Alexander won't always be there to save you."

I almost let my smile slip, but regained my composure quickly. Alexander *had* been saving my ass a lot recently. "I don't need saving."

He grunted and stormed off.

We all stood around awkwardly for a moment until Jackson cleared his throat. "Well, that was fun."

I eyed him. "Your dad's a dick."

"Tell me something I don't know," he mumbled and walked

over to Bash. I followed him and Bash pulled me into a one-arm embrace. He smelled like a mixture of the woods and his soap. He must have just shifted.

"How did Oliver do?" he murmured into my hair as he kissed the top of my head.

"Why don't you see for yourself?" I pulled him towards the house and Bash and Jackson followed me down the hallway to the end, where I'd left the door slightly ajar. I pushed it open and we headed down the stairs to find Ollie pacing anxiously inside the cage. His coat bristled at the sight of us. Bash approached the silver cage, keeping his distance to prevent the affects from hitting him. Ollie growled and snarled at him, adding a sharp, barking sound as he snapped his canines.

"Bad pup," Jackson teased, and I elbowed him.

"He's not a pup," I grumbled and watched Bash as he stared Ollie down.

"Heel," Bash demanded, and I tensed. *What is he doing?* My brother growled defiantly and I took a step forward, but Jackson held me back, shaking his head, silently letting me know not to interfere. "Oliver Grey, heel!" Sebastian's voice boomed in the basement and I felt a chill run down my spine. He was in full Alpha mode.

Ollie stilled, his amber eyes glowing as he stared into Bash's sapphire eyes. Suddenly, he plopped down, laid at Bash's feet, and started to whine.

I tugged on Jackson's hold, but it was firm and he wouldn't release me. I wanted to go to Ollie. For some reason, I felt compelled to stop this.

"He's not you," Jackson whispered in my ear. "Oliver must be initiated just like everyone else."

30

"Shift!" Bash commanded, and I felt the power exuding from him. It was strong and directed straight toward Ollie.

Before our eyes, my brother shifted back into his human form. It was a little messy and painful at times, but once he got the hang of it, it would be easy. After a few minutes he was lying on the concrete, naked and sweaty, breathing heavily.

I ripped myself from Jackson and grabbed the blanket on the table and ran toward the cage. I was about to open it when Bash extended his arm over my chest and stopped me.

"He's a big boy, Mackenzie. Leave him."

My mouth fell open, but nothing came out. I looked over at Ollie, heartbroken to see he could barely lift his head on his own. I clutched the blanket tightly against my chest, slapping Bash's arm away. Jackson steered me to the side and away from the power struggle unfolding before us.

Sebastian opened the cage door but didn't go inside. He knelt on one knee and beckoned Ollie over. My brother dragged himself over with trembling arms. I couldn't stand seeing him like this.

"Oliver, you have completed your first full shift," Bash said, his voice neutral. "Now you must join a Pack. I have petitioned for you to join mine. If you accept—"

"Wait a fuckin' minute!" I exclaimed and flung the blanket across the room. "Who the hell said he wanted to join a Pack?"

"Kenz," Jackson started as he tried to calm me down.

I pulled away from him defiantly. "Don't *Kenz* me." I squatted down beside a frustrated Bash and looked at my brother. "Ollie, listen to me, you don't have to do anything you don't want to do. If you want to be free, you can be a lone wolf. Joining a Pack isn't your only option, no matter if that's how they present it. I'm a lone wolf."

"You're a MacCoinnich," Bash scoffed. "Your case is different. It's still not safe for lone wolves. He's better off joining a Pack. You know this, Mackenzie. Don't make this difficult."

I bit my lower lip and stared at my big brother. I only wanted what was best for him. Bash's Pack wasn't bad, but at the end of the day they were still Pack. Men had it better, but Ollie was coming from a human life where he had choices. In a Pack culture, they would tell him what to do—what his occupation would be, who he could mate with, everything. The Lycan had their whole lives to learn to be okay with that. My brother didn't.

"Kenzie," Ollie said breathlessly. He picked himself up and leaned on his elbow. "Sebastian has already explained everything to me. He told me what you've done, and I think you're amazing."

"But ... ?" I said, blinking rapidly to hold back the tears.

"But I come from a structured environment in the military. I believe in teamwork and family, and I can get all that from the Pack. I also know the downsides. Sebastian didn't hold back when he told me the good, bad, and the ugly. I'll be okay."

Bash reached for my hand and squeezed tightly. "I'll take care of him, Mackenzie. You have my word."

I nodded silently, because there wasn't much else I could say. I had to respect his decision. It wasn't mine to make, and he knew what he was getting into. That was the important part. He wasn't going in blind.

4

Scrubbing the toilet bowl really gave you a whole new perspective on life. In other words, I decided to get a cleaning lady because living with guys made this chore traumatic.

"None of you are allowed to use this bathroom!" I shouted from the downstairs bathroom as I waved the toilet brush in the air.

Bash popped his head inside. "Don't complain. When I cleaned *our* bathroom, I pulled a wig out of the shower drain."

"Shut up!" I glowered at him and threw the brush at his face, but he ducked just in time.

I heard his laugh all the way upstairs and I hurried up to finish cleaning. We were getting the house ready for Alexander's arrival, which should be in about two hours, depending on traffic. It was all-hands-on-deck for this behemoth of a house and I was exhausted.

After we left Cadwell Estate, Ollie shifted a couple more

times, but he mainly rested because the first shift took a lot out of him. Unfortunately, I now had him cleaning my house. Eventually, he would have to move into the Compound since he was now Pack, but I convinced Bash to give us a few days since Alexander was coming to visit.

I put away the cleaning supplies and hurried upstairs to shower and get ready while the guys got ready themselves. When I was dressed and presentable, I met everyone downstairs where they were waiting in the living room.

"So, let me get this straight," Ollie said as he sat in the armchair wearing a pair of pressed slacks and a dress shirt with shiny black shoes. "Your bio-dad is the King, you're pretty much royalty, and you're greeting him looking like *that*?" He pointed at me.

I looked down at my attire. I was wearing my good jeans, a clean gray tank top, and I was still wearing a pair of cheap flip flops.

"What's wrong with what I'm wearing?"

Bash grinned. "This is why I love you."

My eyes narrowed. "Liar."

He shrugged. "I grew to love it." He grabbed my wrist and pulled me down to sit beside him on the sofa, wrapping his arm around me. "But Oliver is correct. Don't you want to dress up a little to see your father?"

"He's not going to care what I'm wearing. Only you losers give a shit, which is why you're wearing your monkey suits."

It was a great honor to have a visit from King Alexander MacCoinnich, but I thought by now the awe would have worn off. At least for Bash. To be fair, Ollie was meeting him for the first time. The two of them looked like it was Sunday and they were going to church.

The doorbell rang and we sat up straighter. It could only be one person.

"I'll get the door," Bash announced as he stood and went to answer.

Now I started to get nervous. My hands got clammy and I had to rub them on my jean-clad thighs. Ollie blew out a breath and sat at the edge of his seat in anticipation. We looked at one another and knew what the other was thinking—*this is going to be crazy!* We chuckled and jumped up when we heard Alexander's Scottish brogue enter the living room.

"It's wonderful to see ye, Sebastian," Alexander said as he clapped him on the back.

"Likewise, Your Highness," Bash said, coming around to stand in the middle of the room.

"Please, I've told ye, call me Alexander."

"Of course." Bash nodded. "Alexander, I'd like to introduce you to our newest Pack member and Mackenzie's brother, Oliver Grey." He motioned toward my brother.

Ollie knelt on one knee, placed a fist over his heart, and bowed his head. "Your Highness."

My jaw dropped. *What the fuck? How the hell did he know to do that? And how is my brother better at being a Lycan than I am?* This would be hilarious if I wasn't mildly offended.

"Rise," Alexander commanded. Ollie stood, standing at attention like a soldier. My father had to look up to stare at Ollie because he was so tall, but he observed every aspect of Ollie's face, almost like he was memorizing it. "I can see a slight resemblance, but ye take after yer parents, lad." He patted Ollie on the arm and turned to me. "Darling."

I stared into those gray eyes that were identical to mine, other than some wrinkles on the corners, as he smiled at me. His dark hair was peppered with a few more white hairs, but even with those minor age factors, he still looked so young. And I looked so much like him.

"Hey Alexander." I smiled and met him halfway. He pulled me into a tight embrace and squeezed me as if he feared I wasn't real. He smelled freshly showered, even though he'd been traveling all day, and I sighed into his arms. Although I hadn't wanted him to come, relief washed over me and I didn't want to let him go.

"It's good to see ye, darling. Ye look good," he muttered into my hair.

"You're looking older," I mumbled.

A laugh rumbled out of him and it vibrated through me. He pulled back, still holding me by my arms. "Aye, the years have nae been kind to me. A lot of stress, but don ye worry about it."

He didn't have to tell me about it; it was all about the aftermath of the Freedom War. Some Packs were still fighting back, some needed to be disciplined, new leadership needed to be placed, and treaties had to be written. Nothing that could be done overnight. I started the war, but then left it for Alexander to deal with. It made me feel so guilty. He told me not to worry, that my time was coming very soon, but I saw the stress he was under. I certainly didn't make it any better with all the shit I added on.

"Have ye forgot about *me*, Princess?" Ranulf said from behind Alexander.

I shrieked. "Ranulf!" Jumping out of Alexander's embrace, I

ran over to the King's right-hand man. I leapt onto him and he caught me easily.

"Ye stupid girl," he grumbled affectionately.

"Oddly enough, I missed that." I climbed off him, grinning wildly. "Did you miss *me*?"

"Hell no," he grunted, but gave me a sly smile.

I poked his chest. "I know you did, you grumpy old man." My gaze traveled the room and I found three other guards standing by the door and living room entrance. They didn't travel light. "You came with an entourage," I said as I went to stand beside Bash and Ollie.

"As King, I cannae travel alone." Alexander gave me a look that said this was the future I had to look forward to.

"Your guards have been set up with their own rooms at the Compound, which is around the corner from here," Bash said. "If you wish to get settled—"

Alexander held up a hand, interrupting him. "I would like for my daughter and I to go get some real New York pizza."

The last time he was there, he ditched his security detail the minute he landed, and we went out for pizza at a place near my apartment. I supposed we were making this a tradition.

"Well, damn." I looked around the room at the others, then my gaze landed on Alexander. "What are we waiting for?"

He clapped his hands together. "That's my girl." Alexander took off his suit jacket and tie, handing it over to Ranulf. "We'll be back, gentlemen." He gave me his arm and I slipped mine in his. "Shall we?"

We left the house without another word, and I was pretty sure everyone was a little more than confused about the sudden turn of events. They expected to get right down to business, when

Alex just wanted some one-on-one time with me. So much for the monkey suits.

I walked us down the street, on the opposite side of the Compound, and down a couple blocks to a small mom and pop shop I discovered a few days ago. It didn't have any place you could sit, but there was a counter where you could stand and eat. When we got there, we ordered two slices each and the grease was seeping off the white paper plates. That was how you knew it was good. With two sodas, we stood at the counter and prepared to dig in.

Alexander unbuttoned his sleeves and rolled them up. "I've missed this, darling." He grinned at me. "We don have pizza like this in Scotland."

I grabbed some napkins and handed a couple to him. "I'm sure you do, you just haven't found it yet."

"Aye, but it's worth the trip, lass." He winked at me and took a big bite of his pizza.

We ate in relative silence, talking about non-important things in between bites, and then he went back for seconds.

"So, we can't avoid the topic forever. What is it you want to ask me, Alexander?" I leaned against the counter and gave him a knowing look.

"That obvious, lass?"

"Very," I chuckled. "But don't worry, I wanted to get out of the house anyway."

"I really *did* want pizza, but yer right, I wanted to talk to ye about yer brother—"

"I'm really sorry, Alexander! I'm truly sorry, I didn't mean—"

He placed a gentle hand on my shoulder. "Darling, I'm nae mad at ye."

I raised a brow and tilted my head. "You're not?"

He grinned and shook his head. "No. Was it rash? Aye. But I understand why ye did it."

I sputtered. "Then why are you here?" None of this made sense. I thought he was here to reprimand me. He hadn't sounded very happy on the phone.

"Do I need a reason to see my daughter?"

I rolled my eyes and laughed. "I guess not."

"Ye've gone through a lot, lass, and I just want to be here for ye. Let me support ye."

Looking at it from his point of view, things had been a little crazy over on this side of the pond. First Enzo, then I lost my wolf, then the whole thing with the vampires, getting kidnapped and tortured, followed by that mess when Bobby Wu bound himself to me, and then I topped it off by biting my brother. And that was just the Cliff notes version! Yeah, one could say I'd been put through the ringer lately. I was due for a break.

I stared into Alexander's caring eyes and couldn't say no even if I wanted to. He really wanted to be a father to me, and I wouldn't make it hard for him. After all he'd done, it wouldn't be fair.

"Thank you, Alexander." I smiled, and he squeezed my arm before letting go.

"Now tell me, darling, how do ye feel about yer brother being a Lycan?"

I shrugged. "I don't know. I'm nervous, I guess. I have a lot of enemies. When people find out he's my brother, they might go after him. Am I being too paranoid?"

"Nae at all. Family can be a strength, but they can also be a weakness. I worry all the time about ye."

I frowned. "You think someone would ever use me against you?"

He nodded. "Aye. I don think, I *know* someday it will happen. And there isn't anything I would nae do to keep ye safe."

"Weakness," I mumbled. "How do we keep the people we love safe?"

Alexander sighed. "If I could hide ye away in Castle Mac, I would, Mackenzie." He chuckled. "But I cannae. I just have to trust that ye'll take care of yerself. Even if ye put yerself in such crazy situations," he mumbled the last part.

I winced and smiled. "Sorry."

"Oliver will be fine, darling. Don worry." He pulled me into a hug.

It was hard not to worry. Worry was my middle name at this point.

"Speaking of family," I began, clearing my throat and stepping back, "I learned some things about Adaline ..."

He tensed. "Oh?"

That was all he had to say? I literally just spoke the name of his soulmate and all I got was *oh?* Men were so weird.

"Yeah, I paid a visit to the archivist to learn more about Oracles and found, like, a registry, I think. It had the date she was born and where, plus her parents' name and some other stuff. Do you ... do you know if they're still alive?"

Alexander ran a hand through his dark hair, the curl on his forehead flipping back. Worry lines formed on his temple. "Last I checked, they were still alive. Do ye wish to meet them?"

I gnawed on the corner of my bottom lip. "I don't know. Do they even know I exist?"

He shook his head. "I don believe so, lass. Yer mum almost

took that secret to her grave. But if ye want to meet them, I will make it happen, darling. Anything ye want."

I nodded. "Thank you, Alexander. I'll keep that in mind. In the meantime, would you like to meet my adoptive parents?"

He grinned. "I thought ye'd never ask! Of course I would, lass."

"Good!" I laughed. "We're having dinner this weekend with Ollie and I'd like for you to be there. But remember, they don't know anything about me, and especially not about what happened to Ollie. So just pretend you're some rich guy from Scotland."

"Aye, I can do that."

I'd have to figure out a way to break it to my parents that Alexander was coming to dinner as well. They wouldn't be upset, but my mother would freak out and start planning an elaborate meal. Nothing about this dinner would be easy.

"How's Lucian?" I asked as we started to head out of the pizza shop and walk back to my house.

Alexander smiled. "He's well, darling. Misses ye dearly." That only made me feel worse. I missed him, too. More than I ever expected.

"I swear I'll fix it," I muttered.

Alexander wrapped an arm around me as we walked. "I know ye will, but he does nae blame ye. Don be so hard on yerself. Lucian is his own man and he made his own choices, remember that."

But he wouldn't have had to make them if it wasn't for me.

WE MADE it back to the house and when we did, the guards had already been taken to the Compound, including Ranulf. Bash was in the living room watching TV, obviously waiting up for us, but Alexander was tired and I escorted him to the other guestroom so he could go to sleep.

I went back downstairs and quietly sat on the sofa. Bash was practically vibrating with the need to know what happened while we were gone. And just to torture him a little longer, I kept quiet and even yawned, stretching my arms wide, hinting I was tired.

"Seriously, Mackenzie?"

I innocently looked his way. "What?" I gave him my best doe eyes.

"You know what. What happened?"

I grinned slyly. "You're so nosy, wanting all the gossip."

"Mackenzie," he growled.

I raised my hands in surrender. "Okay, okay. We just talked a little about Ollie. He told me he wasn't mad at me, which I'm super surprised at, then we talked about my bio-mom and her parents, and I asked about Lucian. Honestly, it was really a personal conversation. None of it had anything to do with you." I bopped him on the nose.

"He didn't tell you why he was here?" Bash raised a brow.

"Because he wants to spend time with me." I shrugged. "There's no ulterior motive, Bash." I climbed over him and straddled him, unbuttoning his shirt. "Now, no more talking."

"Mackenzie, your father is upstairs. So is your brother." He placed his hands on my hips to keep me steady.

"And they're tucked away in bed, boy scout. Chill."

"I'm nae in bed just yet, darling," Alexander said from the stairs that overlooked the living room.

I jumped off Sebastian like he had lice and scooted as far away on the sofa as I could get. Why did we always get caught in the most compromising positions?

"Alexander," Bash grunted as he stood, a blush creeping up his neck. He hurried to button up his shirt again. "Our apologies—"

"Relax, Sebastian." Alexander motioned for him to sit back down as he walked toward us. "I only came down for a glass of water." He was dressed in a pair of striped pajamas and slippers. It was adorable.

"You're welcome to anything in the kitchen," I said with a tight smile. My adoptive father had never caught me with a boy, but Alexander had managed to catch me twice now. It was a conspiracy, I tell you.

He was about to head to the kitchen when he thought better of it and turned toward us.

"Have ye two thought about mating yet?" Alexander asked casually, causing me to choke on my own spit.

"What?!" I exclaimed, my eyes wide in horror. I looked at Bash, but he wouldn't acknowledge me. He was sitting on the edge of the sofa; his elbows were on his knees and he was staring at the ground.

"Sebastian?" Alexander called him and his head popped up.

I didn't understand what I was seeing—was Bash actually sad? His shoulders were slumped in defeat and I could see in his ocean blue eyes, this was something he wanted but didn't think he'd ever get. And I bet my reaction didn't help. I was the absolute worst.

"Yes, Alexander?" There was a crackle in his voice I'd never heard before.

"Have ye thought about it?"

He sighed. "*I* have, but this isn't something Mackenzie wants."

"What is it *ye* want, Sebastian?" Alexander asked. I was frozen in my seat.

"It doesn't matter—"

"It matters." My eyes were so wide, I felt like they were going to pop out of my head. "You really want this?" I whispered.

"You don't understand, Mackenzie," Bash said. "This is a very important rite of passage for a Lycan. It's extremely rare for us to have an Anam, so to not seal it with a mating bond, it just doesn't feel whole."

"You should have told me," I muttered, unable to look at him.

"You've made it very clear that you're against our traditions."

I stood from the sofa and started to pace the living room. Could I do something like this? It was the equivalent of marriage, and this all sounded like a business transaction with Alexander being the intermediary. Why did he have to say something?

"Some traditions are nae bad, Mackenzie. If ye love him—"

"Why are you ganging up on me?" I blurted. "Maybe I'm just not ready! Have you ever thought about that?"

Alexander rubbed his forehead and ran a hand through his hair. "Mackenzie—"

"Alexander, wait—" Bash shot up from the sofa, stopping him.

I looked between the two of them. They were eyeing each other, having a silent conversation without me.

"What the hell?" I yelled, loud enough that I was sure I woke Ollie. "What don't I know?" I stared at Alexander, who only stared at Bash. Then I remembered what Bash said when I first got home ...

He didn't tell you why he was here?

44

Alexander lied. He wasn't here to spend time with me. "Why are you *really* here?" I asked, my eyes silvering and my fists tightening at my sides.

"I have to tell her," he said to Bash, and then looked down at me. "Mackenzie, have a seat."

"I'd rather stand," I growled.

He sighed and nodded. "Very well." Alexander reached for my hands and I let him hold them in his. "Mackenzie, I love ye dearly. I wish I could give ye the normal life ye desire, but unfortunately that is nae the case." He took a deep breath and squeezed my hands. "I'll be stepping down from the crown soon."

I frowned. "I know."

"I don't think you understand, Mackenzie," Bash said. "He's stepping down *soon*."

I tensed and tried to pull away, but Alexander wouldn't let me go. "How soon?"

"In six months, darling."

A chill coursed through my normally hot body and I felt extremely lightheaded. The corner of my eyes dimmed, and the room started to tilt. I began to sway, and if Alexander hadn't been holding on to me, I surely would have dropped to the ground like a block of cement.

"Mackenzie!" Bash called out, but he sounded so far away.

I stared into the distance and felt someone shake me. "Lassie, look at me!" Alexander shouted and my head snapped in his direction.

"What?" I mumbled.

"Bloody hell, I thought ye were going to pass out. Did ye hear what I said?"

"She's in shock." Bash grabbed me by my shoulders, pulling

me backwards until I fell on the sofa. "Mackenzie, you knew this time would come."

I gulped. "But six months?" I peered up at Alexander who stood in front of me. "You told me I had time."

"The Council and the Summits are pushing me out." He squatted before me, placing his hands on my knees. "It's why I'm here, darling. I wanted to tell ye in person without the prying ears of others."

"Why are they pushing you out? I don't understand," I said in a daze.

"The Council and the Summits do nae like the changes being made. They like the old ways, but they can nae overrule me, so they want ye on the throne to challenge ye for the position. If that happens, the MacCoinnichs will lose the crown after holding it for a thousand years."

My face turned into a scowl. "They really think it'll be that easy?"

Alexander smirked. "Aye. But they don know ye, lass. Nae like I do." He squeezed my knee.

"Why did you bring up the mating bond, then?" I frowned, still not understanding.

He sighed. "Unfortunately, this is still politics, and ye need to show a united front. If ye and Sebastian are mated, ye'll be stronger than ever. It'll be harder for them to dethrone ye."

I *knew* this was a business transaction. Well, for Alexander it was. Bash, on the other hand, wanted this because he wanted to be with me.

"How did you know?" I turned to Bash, who was sitting beside me.

"It was announced at the last Summit meeting," he admitted.

"I'm normally not there since it's only for the region Alphas, but I had something to report that day. I only learned about Alexander stepping down; I didn't know about the Council and Summits' plans."

"I swore him to secrecy, darling, because I wanted to be the one to tell ye," Alexander said. "It was only right that ye hear it from me."

This was all too much, not to mention horrible timing. I had six months to enjoy my freedom before it was gone, and then I'd have to battle the Council and Summits just to stay in power—a power I didn't even want. No wonder Charles said I wouldn't last. He already knew about their plans for me.

Being Queen was the last thing I ever wanted to be, but I'd be damned if I let them take it away from the MacCoinnich family.

I steeled myself as I stared unflinchingly at Alexander. "I'll do whatever it takes. They're not getting that crown."

5

I slept like shit that night. Anxiety ate at me and I could barely stay asleep for more than an hour before waking up and having to go splash water on my face. Eventually I gave up and headed downstairs to watch Netflix until it was time to get ready for work. It was obvious when I walked into the squad room that I'd had a rough night.

"Whoa, Grey, you sure you want to be here today?" Michaels asked as he looked at me from across his desk.

"I'm fine," I mumbled and stuffed my bag in my bottom desk drawer.

"Did you even comb your hair?" Finn asked from across the room.

"Mind your business, Reaper!" He chuckled and I heard him shuffle out of the squad room.

Cas came out of Briggs's office while I was booting up my computer and did a double take when he saw me, then came straight to my desk, sitting on top of it.

"Something you need to get off your chest?" he said.

I sighed heavily. "God, I know I look like crap, no need to keep reminding me! I'm fine!"

"You don't sound fine," Cas whispered. "Is this about your dad?"

I scowled. "What do you know about Alexander?"

Cas leaned closer. "I heard my Alpha say he was in town. I figured his visit was probably stressing you out."

My shoulders visibly relaxed. "No, he's not stressing me out. Alexander is staying with me and Bash, so it wasn't a surprise."

"That's good." Cas nodded. "Your dad is cool peeps. You should bring him into the office. I'm sure he'd enjoy a ride-a-long."

I snorted. "Yeah, I'm sure he would. And then he'd make me quit the minute he found out how dangerous this job can be."

"Aw, come on, he's not that bad. He would have pulled you out by now if he was like that."

Cassidy did have a point. Alexander also mentioned he trusted I could take care of myself, so maybe I wasn't giving him enough credit.

"You know what I could use right now?" I got up from my chair and started to pull my hair into a ponytail.

"What's up, Grey?"

"A sparring session. Let me kick your ass, Chang." I pushed him, and he laughed.

"Oh, you're so on! Meet you in the gym in ten!"

Cas hurried to his desk to take off his utility belt and gun and lock it up, and I was digging through my drawers for gym clothes when someone burst through the squad room.

"I need help!" Maximos shouted as he was followed by an

officer in uniform from downstairs. "You!" he pointed at me. "You need to help me."

I snorted. "Are you kidding me? The last time I tried to help you, I almost got written up. Hell, no. Whatever mess you got yourself in, handle it yourself. Or better yet, get your connections up top to help you." I ignored him and snatched up some clothes when he grabbed my arm.

"They stole the Draupnir," he whispered conspiratorially.

"They stole what?" I said loud enough for the others to hear.

He grimaced. "Odin's ring."

I rolled my eyes. "Right, and they're coming for me pot 'o gold next," I said with a shitty Irish accent.

His grip on me tightened. "I'm not making this up, Curse Breaker. This is serious."

"What's serious is the fact that you're going to get your hand off me." My eyes silvered.

Maximos released me immediately. "You may not believe me, but you *will* help me."

Briggs's door opened and the short, bald lieutenant stormed out of his office with a red face, glaring at Maximos. "Grey!" he yelled. "Maximos Limogiannis is top priority. I want you and Chang on the case. Clear everything else on your load." Before I could frame a snappy retort, he marched back into his office and slammed the door.

"Told you." Maximos grinned, his greasy hair slicked back.

"What the hell?" Cas yelled, throwing his hands in the air.

"Watch him," I told Cas, pointing at Maximos.

I hurried to Briggs's office, not bothering to knock, and barged in, closing the door behind me. Briggs was sitting at his desk with his head in his hands, not looking my way.

"What's going on, boss?" I said tentatively as I stepped closer.

"For fuck's sake, Grey. Just do your job," Briggs grumbled.

"Not until you tell me why we're helping that fucker. Especially since he didn't want our help originally. I don't like being toyed with."

Briggs picked his head up and motioned for me to sit down. I took a seat and he cleared his throat. "He called the Commissioner. My hands are tied."

"But the Commissioner is human—"

"Doesn't matter. The SIU is ultimately still run by him. From what I gather, a ring is missing. When you reported to the call at The Third Eye, it was in the vault, but the would-be thieves never got to it. The ring was moved to a secure location, or at least they thought it was, but now it's gone."

I leaned forward. "Maximos called it Draupnir. He said it was Odin's ring. I can't get a serious answer from him. Briggs, I can't work under these conditions. I'm not going to be chasing after some comic book character."

Briggs stared at me for a very uncomfortable moment before nodding. "Do the best you can, Grey," he grumbled. "Use all the resources you need, including Michaels and Finn, but I want you and Cas running point. The sooner we solve this, the better. I want the Commissioner off our backs."

"You got it." I left the office.

Maximos was sitting by my desk with Cassidy hovering near him, and it was obvious he was beyond furious. The feeling was mutual.

I pulled Cas to the side and he told me everything Maximos told him, which only echoed what he already told me and what Briggs just shared. We needed to press him for more details.

"If you want our help," I said as I walked over to Maximos, "we want full disclosure. It's the only way this works. And no more bogus stories. I don't even care about the stupid ring and what it is, because you're obviously not going to tell me the truth. So, why don't you tell us where you hid it the second time?"

Maximos sat up straighter. "I can't tell you."

I rolled my eyes. "Dude, it's already been stolen! The location doesn't matter anymore."

"If you're not going to help us, we can't help you," Cas supplied, cracking his knuckles like an enforcer.

"I can't tell you, because you won't believe me."

Nothing he was saying was believable, but we had to start somewhere. Maximos sat there in his slacks with suspenders and greasy hair, looking every bit the creep he was. He looked like a crooked business owner. I hated that he had the SIU in his pocket.

"Give me your best shot." I leaned against my desk. "Where was the ring being hidden?"

He worried his hands before pulling a handkerchief from his pocket and dabbing his sweaty forehead. "At the Metropolitan Museum of Art. I placed it on display."

My jaw slacked. "You placed it in the Met?"

He nodded. "I thought hiding it in plain sight would be safest. No one would think to check there—"

"You were dead wrong about *that*," Cas grunted. "Who else knew you were putting it there?"

"No one. Only me. Well, and the curator at the Met, but I trust her completely—"

"Mistake number one." I motioned for him to get up. "Come on, let's go."

I went to grab my bag from my drawer, leaving my gun and utility belt behind. Hopefully we wouldn't encounter any trouble. The ring was the trouble, and now it was gone.

"Where are we going?" Maximos asked as he stood, looking around at Cas and me as we got ready.

"We're going to the museum," Cassidy said. "We need to check out the security footage of the theft. Once we find out who we're dealing with, we'll have a better idea how to handle this."

Maximos didn't argue with us as we left the squad room, not bothering to see if he was following or not. Cas and I were like a well-oiled machine as we headed out of the SIU building and aimed straight for the unmarked cop car. I tossed him the keys and he caught them easily over on the other side of the car. He unlocked it and we climbed inside, waiting only a split second for Maximos to get in. We were leaving with or without him.

We rolled down the windows and Cas pulled out onto the busy city street. Blazing hot air filled the car and the breeze was too warm to cool us down. It was worse for wolves. Halfway through the drive to the Upper East Side, I was airing out my shirt as sweat glistened on my skin.

"They need to get the A/C in this car fixed soon," I groaned.

"It's not so bad," Maximos said.

I turned around from the passenger seat and glared at him. "No one asked you."

Cas chuckled. "They put the order in. We should get a car from another precinct next week."

Besides my occasional complaining, we made it to the Met in no time and parked at the parking garage on Fifth avenue and Eightieth street. I hadn't been to the museum since I was a kid on a school field trip, so I followed Cassidy's lead as he flashed his badge at the front desk and requested to speak with the head of security.

"Who is the curator you spoke with?" I asked Maximos while Cas dealt with the employees.

"Her name is Ann Leblanc. She's one of us," he whispered the last part. "She's fae."

"Call her," I said sternly. When he didn't move, I practically dug through his pockets myself for his phone.

"Okay, okay! Relax, Curse Breaker," he mumbled.

"Stop calling me that. My name is Mackenzie. Use it."

The sound of high heels resonated against the floor and I looked up just in time to see a beautiful woman with a blonde bob swaying side-to-side, reaching out to shake Cassidy's hand. Her bright, blood-red lips were spread in a smile I couldn't quite place, and she was dressed like a businesswoman. A very fashionable one. I looked down at my raggedy jeans and t-shirt and then looked back at her. We were total polar opposites.

"That's her," Maximos muttered as he passed me and then spread his arms out wide. "Ann, darling!"

"Mr. Limogiannis." Her smile tightened. "If you were planning to involve the SIU, a heads-up would have been preferable."

I adjusted my messy hair before stepping in. "The SIU's involvement should have been obvious, Miss ...?"

"Leblanc," she said, her piercing eyes hitting me. "I still like to be notified of things that involve my place of employment. You can understand that, surely."

"Of course," Cas said, giving me side eye. "But since we're here, would it be too much trouble to request the security footage of the theft?"

She smiled brightly at Cas and took in his large frame. "It

wouldn't be too much trouble. I want this resolved as quickly as possible. I'm sure you do as well."

"*We* do," I said, clearing my throat. "Actually, Miss Leblanc, was there anyone you might have told about the ring being in the museum's possession?"

"Excuse me?" she said, taken aback. "You think *I* could be at fault here?" Her hand went to her chest to clutch at imaginary pearls and her eyes darted to Cas, then back to me.

"That's not what I said at all—"

"We just want to know if anyone else knew," Cas interjected, since it seemed she had a thing for him. *Ew, gross.*

She flattened her hand on her stomach and stretched out her neck. "Not at all. I told no one. And I kept it locked in a location only I have access to."

"Thank you, Miss Leblanc," I said. "You've been a tremendous help. Would you mind showing us the footage now?"

She nodded and waved us down toward an employee-only area. Ann and Cas walked ahead of us and I could hear her talking to him about what she did at the Met, really talking herself up. I couldn't tell if Cas was into her or not, but I didn't get a bad vibe from her. She was just a little snooty, which was typical in the fae, so I wasn't surprised. Cassidy needed someone in his life. But I wasn't going to play cupid.

We were walking down a hallway when I caught a familiar scent. I couldn't place it, but I'd smelled it somewhere before. I paused in the middle of the hallway and Maximos stopped with me.

"What is it, Curse—Mackenzie?"

"Uh ... I don't know. Go ahead and catch up with the others. I'll be there shortly."

Maximos thought about it for a moment before leaving me behind. When they were a far distance away, I opened my senses and sniffed the area. It was almost like I smelled tea, which honestly was a weird thing to smell. I was a coffee drinker and was never around tea.

I retraced my steps, but when I didn't catch anything, I decided it was all in my head. I started to walk back to the others when a door opened behind me and I was yanked inside. My body was slammed against the wall and a hand clamped over my mouth.

The room was pitch black, but I could feel a hard body pressed against me, pinning me to the wall and locking my arms so I couldn't move. My eyes silvered and I switched to night vision to get a good look at my surroundings. It was a room full of art, neatly packaged, that was either being shipped out or had just shipped in. But in front of me was a very familiar face.

It was the man Bobby Wu took me to see.

"Promise you won't scream?" he said in his somewhat British accent. Those dark eyes drilled into me and his intent was clear: if I screamed, he'd kill me. And I was pretty sure he could.

I growled deep in my throat before nodding.

"Good." He grinned and removed his hand from my mouth, but didn't release me. "Now we can have a proper chat."

"What the hell are you doing here?" I snarled, pushing against his hold.

"Wouldn't you like to know?" he smirked. "What *I'd* like to know is what *you* are doing here?"

"Wouldn't you like to know?" I mimicked.

"Smart arse," he grumbled. "Now, Mackenzie, where is Bobby? He has not been returning my calls."

I could have been cocky about it and bragged about capturing him with my typical Mackenzie flare, but I decided it would be wiser to heed Bobby's warnings—this man was dangerous and could kill me easily. I had to be careful and not provoke him. Whoever *he* was.

I shrugged. "I don't know where he is. He disappeared a couple weeks ago."

He took the collar of my shirt with the strap of my bra and pulled it over my shoulder, exposing my skin roughly, where Bobby Wu's handprint once was.

"Where's your mark?"

"I told you." I glared. "I'm resourceful."

His hand tightened on my shirt collar, stretching it out and rumpling it. If Bash were here, watching this, he'd have a freakin' fit.

"Will you get the fuck off me?" I nudged him. If he pulled my shirt any lower, it would expose my chest and then I wouldn't give a damn, I'd wolf out in the middle of the Met.

He released my shirt but didn't let me go. "If I find out you had anything to do with Bobby's disappearance—"

"You'll what?" I jerked my head. "Kill me? I don't even know who you are."

His grin widened. "You can call me Úlfur."

I choked on a laugh. "Úlfur? What?"

"You laugh now, but you won't be laughing for long, little wolf," he whispered. His weight laid off me a bit and I could breathe better. "You're right to fear me. You'd be stupid if you didn't. I know Bobby told you as much."

I schooled my expression, but wondered how he knew that I feared him. Did I? He made me nervous, but was that fear? No. It could have been something Bobby told him about me. I was reading too much into it.

"I'll be watching you, Mackenzie Grey. Whatever you've done—"

"I didn't do anything!" I whisper-shouted. "I told you, Bobby disappeared. He was nervous about something. I don't know what it was. Maybe it was you."

Those ebony eyes pierced me in place, trying to find the lie I spoke, but I only stared into his eyes, never breaking contact. I wasn't going to give him any reason to doubt me. There was no way he could find out what we did to the warlock.

He sighed. "If you're after the ring, you're too late. Why are you after it?"

"Why do you think? I thought you knew all about me. I'm a cop, it's my job."

Úlfur leaned closer, placing his mouth to my ear and I tensed. "Stop searching, little wolf. It's not time yet."

Before I could say anything, Úlfur slammed his head into mine and everything went black.

6

"Kenz!" Cassidy's voice rang through my pounding head and I felt a subtle shake of my shoulders. "Come on, Grey, wake up."

I groaned, reaching for my forehead and wincing when I touched a sore spot. "What the hell?" I mumbled.

"Thank God."

I opened my eyes and found Cas squatted in front of me. I was sitting on the ground, leaning against the wall. My gaze traveled around the room and I realized I was still in the same room Úlfur pulled me into, but now the lights were on and Ann and Maximos were by the door waiting.

"What happened?" I muttered as I tried to get up, flinching when a sharp pain shot through my head.

"I was hoping you could tell me, Kenz. I found you in here, passed out with that lump on your head."

What happened was that I was head-butted by Úlfur and his head was like a boulder. It was beyond supernatural for him to

59

knock me out with that blow and leave him standing. What the hell was he?

"I was attacked, but I didn't see who it was," I lied.

"I guess a lot of that is going around," Cas sighed. "The security footage was stolen. We got nothing."

Was that why Úlfur was here? Did he have something to do with this? I must not have reacted the way Cas expected, because he raised a suspicious brow and I shook my head.

"Sorry." I rubbed my head. "I think I'm concussed."

"Of course. Shit. Sorry, Grey. Let's head back to the station and get you looked at," he said as he helped me stand.

Cassidy took Ann's information down in case we needed to follow up and we told Maximos to go home. There was nothing we could do until we got another lead.

I hobbled my way back to the car, leaning on Cas, and then we paid for parking and drove back to the SIU. Throughout the ride, Cas peppered me with as many questions as he would a witness to a homicide, but I couldn't answer any of them. When we walked into the squad room, I squinted against the fluorescent lights and aimed straight for my desk.

"What happened to you?" Michaels shot up and came around my desk. His calloused fingers brushed against my forehead. "Who did this?" he asked in his gruff New York accent.

"I didn't get a good look," I mumbled, avoiding eye contact.

"Well, you might want to rethink that answer," Michaels whispered, leaning forward. "Your father is in Briggs's office with his guard."

My head snapped up and I flinched from the pain. "And you're just *now* telling me?"

Michaels shrugged. "I thought you'd have a better answer

than *I didn't get a good look,*" he deadpanned. "Go see the witches and get yourself cleaned up before they come out."

I grimaced as I tried to stand, and Cas and Michaels helped me as I wobbled on my feet. Just as I was about to take my first step, Briggs's office door opened.

"Shit," I murmured. "Turn me around." We shuffled around, presenting them with my back, and the two of them covered by hiding me behind them.

"Wonderful talking to ye, Lieutenant. Please stay in contact—ah, Cassidy, my boy! How are ye?" Alexander shouted from a distance. I could hear his footsteps getting closer.

"Your Highness," Cas's voice boomed with pride and I imagined him straightening before Alexander.

There was a pregnant pause before someone cleared their throat.

"Bow before yer King!" Ranulf yelled, and I realized Cas hadn't taken a knee to keep me hidden behind him.

Shit. I couldn't keep hiding behind him and getting him in trouble. That was just selfish. I turned around just as Cas was about to say something and placed a hand on his arm.

"Bow," I whispered.

Cassidy relaxed in my hold and dropped to a knee, placing a fist over his heart and bowing his head before his King, exposing me in front of Alexander.

"Mackenzie!" Alexander gasped. "What happened, darling?" I nodded toward Cassidy and he did a double take. "Rise," he said, his gray eyes trailing back to me.

Cas stood and stepped aside to stand beside me, Michaels standing sentinel on my other side.

"We were out in the field and I was attacked. No big deal." I motioned at my head. "Just a little bump on the noggin." I grinned lazily.

Alexander's eyes silvered and he took a step forward, but Ranulf held him back. "I want to know who did this," he demanded coldly.

"I didn't get a good look," I repeated with a sigh. "It's all part of the job, Alexander. Let's not make a fuss."

"Kenz was on her way to see one of the witches," Cassidy said. "She mentioned she might be concussed."

I wanted to choke him in that moment. Let's not add to the drama!

"No! We'll take her home," Alexander said, looking back at Ranulf and motioning him toward me.

"Come now, Princess," Ranulf said as he came to grab my arm.

"You gotta be kidding me," I muttered. "Alexander, I'm a grown woman. You can't do this. I have work to do."

"Mackenzie," he growled. "Do nae argue with me. Yer injured. Ye need to shift, and we're taking ye home. End of discussion."

I could have thrown a tantrum, but honestly my head was throwing the biggest house party known to man and I could barely keep my eyes open. If I tried to argue, I'd probably pass out. Damn Úlfur and his steel forehead. Instead, I shuffled out of the squad room, escorted out by Ranulf and Alexander like a scolded child with my head ducked down in shame. They had a town car idling in front of the SIU building, parked in front of a fire hydrant. Ranulf slid into the passenger seat as Alexander and I sat in the back.

I rested my head against the cool window, grateful for the A/C blasting through the vents. I couldn't take this summer heat any longer.

"What's going on, lass?" Alexander murmured once we pulled into traffic.

"Nothing." I shrugged. "Just working a case."

"Yer mind is someplace else. Ye know more than yer telling."

I swallowed loudly. How could he read me so easily? Was I that predictable?

I turned my head to stare at Alexander. "Do you know someone named Úlfur?" I asked, throwing caution to the wind.

He frowned. "Never heard of that name. Is that who attacked ye?"

I nodded. "This isn't the first time I've met him, but this is the first time I learned his name. The warlock I was bound to used to take me to see him. Úlfur seemed to know a lot about me when we visited him."

Alexander ran a hand across his mouth. "I don like this, darling. If this involves the warlock, it is nae good news."

"But Bobby is gone," I said. "We don't have anything to worry about. I think Úlfur knocked me out so I wouldn't follow him."

"How did he get the jump on ye, Princess?" Ranulf asked from the front seat. "Yer usually quicker on yer feet."

My expression tightened. My ego had taken a substantial hit today. Then again, this guy seemed to be extremely strong. "Truthfully, I didn't see it coming."

We drove the rest of the way to Brooklyn in relative silence with Alexander taking the occasional call from the King's Council that was in the castle to talk business. I couldn't believe what I was listening to. They were already talking about preparing for his departure, and he still had six months left. I was biting my tongue so damn hard I tasted blood. It only made my head hurt more.

When we arrived at the house, instead of going inside, I sat on the steps leading to the front door and told them I'd be inside shortly. Once Ranulf and Alexander were gone, I pulled out my phone and texted Bash.

Less than ten minutes later, he was rounding the corner from the Compound and coming towards me.

"What happened?" he asked as he got closer. I was getting really tired of that question.

"I got a little boo-boo at work. Wanna go shift?"

Bash caressed my face so tenderly, I barely felt his touch. "Of course, Mackenzie."

He didn't ask any more questions as we walked hand-in-hand to Prospect Park, even though I knew he was dying to. He filled me in on his day to avoid the subject of the huge lump on my head and how I got it, and I listened avidly about what had been going on in the Pack.

"I think she has a good chance," Bash said. "Sterling has some of the guys nervous."

I chuckled. "Hell yeah, she does. She's totally going to get that Captain position and make history."

Bash peered down and gave me a small smile. "You're going to revolutionize the Lycans once you take the throne."

I shrugged. "I just want equal rights for the Lunas. It's not really a hard concept to grasp. And the Lycans will learn it, whether they like it or not."

We entered the park and headed for the woods where we normally went on occasions like these. When we found a well-hidden spot away from the public, we started to strip.

"I want to be there for Sterling's fight. Let me know when it is," I said as I pulled my shirt over my head.

"I'm sure she'll tell you herself, but I'll let you know." He unbuttoned his pants and shucked them off.

When we were fully naked, I took our clothes and tucked them somewhere away from prying eyes and met Bash in a clearing where we had space to move. He reached for the back of my head and pulled me toward him, bringing his lips to mine.

"I love you, Mackenzie," he whispered sweetly.

I grinned. "I love you too."

We pulled away and started to shift. It was easy and painless, and within seconds I was on all fours shaking my black coat. My silver eyes narrowed and searched for Bash and I found him behind me, his slate coat bristling and those sapphire eyes glowing as they stared into mine. He strolled toward me, brushing against my side and rubbing his muzzle behind my ear. I turned my head toward him and nudged him back, then I darted for the woods, starting the chase. My paws dug into the soil and I felt the warm breeze ripple against my fur. Pounding steps sounded behind me and I knew Bash was right behind me. I loved it when we played.

I STARED up at the canopy of trees as we laid on the grass, mesmerized by the slivers of blue sky that peeked through the leaves. We'd shifted back about a half hour ago but were too exhausted to move. Several hours had passed as we ran through the woods and I'd already healed. Now we were covered in dirt and leaves and probably a good distance away from our clothes.

I reached for Bash's hand and interlocked our fingers. He sighed.

"Bash?" I said as I watched the trees. There was no breeze, so they weren't moving whatsoever.

"Yes?" I heard the rustle of his head turning to look at me.

I gulped. What I was about to say would change everything, but there was no reason to hold back. It was my own paranoid reservations that kept me from happiness, that kept me from making Bash happy. What did I really have to fear? It wasn't like I never wanted to do it. Eventually I would, so why not now? I found my forever, so why hold back? I shouldn't. I loved him. That was all the reason I needed.

"Mackenzie?" Bash squeezed my hand.

I turned my head to face him. "Will you mate with me?"

His ocean blue eyes widened in a very uncharacteristic way that startled me a bit. Bash wasn't a very animated person.

"What did you say?" He slowly sat up, running a hand through his pitch-black hair, tossing leaves out of it.

"Mate with me," I repeated. "Marry me. Let's do it all." I sat up with him and ran my hand through his hair.

"Mackenzie," he said, slightly out of breath.

"Just say yes, Bash!" I laughed and bit my lower lip.

"Yes," he said mindlessly and pushed me back down on the ground, climbing over me.

His lips crashed onto mine with a ferocity unlike I'd felt before. He wanted to devour me, and I let him. Sebastian's hands roamed my body as if he wanted to touch me all over, all at once. He nestled himself between my legs and slammed inside, and I had to bite down on a moan. This wasn't sweet, it was hungry and rough, and I held onto him as I let him take what he wanted.

"Bash!" I yelled as I dug my nails into his back. I came and the force hit me in waves that left me beyond sensitive. I cried out just as he put his face in the crook of my neck and went over the edge, shuddering above me.

My arms were wrapped around his neck and his chest rose and fell rapidly as he tried to catch his breath. I rubbed soothing circles on his back as I tried to calm my racing heart.

"Mackenzie," his voice cracked. "Don't play with my emotions."

I tightened my hold on him. "I swear I'm not, Sebastian. I promise I want to do this, and for all the right reasons. Not because of some political bullshit, but because I love you and I just don't see any reason not to. And if you want this—"

"I do," he interrupted. "I really do."

"Then we'll do it. Little ceremony, big, I don't care. However you want, it'll happen, but it's about you and me, okay?"

Bash lifted his head and kissed me softly. "You and me."

7

B ash and I were deliriously happy as we walked back to the Compound. I hadn't seen him smile so much since I met him. It was a little concerning, to be honest. I was used to the serious, broody Sebastian Steel. Did I break him?

We entered the Compound and many of the Lycan watched us warily as we walked in. I made a beeline for the kitchen and let Bash go to his office on his own.

"What did you do to him?" Amy marveled as she came up to me from the living room. Her flaming red hair was in a high ponytail with curls that trailed down along her neck. All her tattoos were on full display in her tank top.

"Nothing," I mumbled. "Why would it be *my* fault?" I said, offended.

"Because you have a matching goofy smile, dumbass." She smacked me in the back of the head.

"Ouch!" I rubbed my head. "That was not necessary. Nothing happened, we're just happy."

"Uh huh." She eyed me, not convinced at all. "You can't lie to me, Mackenzie Grey, but I'll allow it since you look so happy." Amy walked over to a cabinet and grabbed a bag of potato chips.

"Enough about me." I snatched the bag from her and grabbed a few chips. "Shouldn't you be shackled to Jackson's bed? I haven't seen you in days."

"Har har." She snatched the bag back. "We've been busy," she said suspiciously, but it was the kind of suspicion I didn't care to find out about. They made their sex life so public, if this was related, God, I didn't want to know!

"Right, you freaks. Well, I gotta go, but we're doing a Netflix night soon!" I said, backing away from the kitchen and taking a water bottle from the fridge.

"I'm counting on it!" she yelled back.

I disappeared from the kitchen and made my way to Bash's office. I passed the living room, walked down the hallway, and knocked twice on the office door before letting myself in. I didn't expect to find Alexander and Ranulf inside.

Alexander was sitting at Bash's desk, Ranulf stood protectively behind him, and Bash was poised on the other side of his desk, his hands clasped behind him like he was being reprimanded.

"What's going on here?" I said as I shut the door behind me.

"Darling, why did ye nae tell me where ye were going?" Alexander said as he leaned on the desk. "After yer attack, I was worried."

I frowned. "I was fine, Alexander. I just went to shift so I could heal. It's not a big deal. I shouldn't have to report my comings and goings."

Alexander's brows furrowed, and it appeared as if he had to

think about that for a moment. He couldn't barge into my life and uproot it, no matter how good his intentions were.

His shoulders relaxed. "My apologies, lass. I'm just nae used to this. Having ye so close makes me very protective."

I sighed. "It's okay, Alexander, but remember, I'm an adult. I don't need daddy's permission to do things."

He perked up when I said *daddy*, and I realized that was probably a poor choice of words. We still weren't there yet. I knew he was waiting for it, but I just wasn't ready. Someday, just not today.

"Did ye have a good shift, at least?" Ranulf interrupted the awkwardness.

I nodded. "I'm all healed up." I walked closer to Bash and looked his way before turning back to Alexander. "There's something we want to tell you."

Bash tensed beside me. I didn't know if he wanted to be the one to tell him or not; we hadn't really talked about sharing the news with anyone, but if there was one person who needed to know, it was Alexander.

"What is it, lass?"

I cleared my throat. "I asked Sebastian to mate with me."

Ranulf choked and I glared at him.

Alexander's gray eyes widened. "Ye did?"

"I did." There was silence as everyone avoided looking at one another. It was kind of a weird reaction, considering how Alexander was practically pushing the issue last night. "What's the problem?"

"Ye do everything so backwards, Princess," Ranulf chuckled. "*Sebastian* was supposed to ask ye."

I threw my hands in the air. "Are you fucking kidding me?"

They couldn't possibly be disgruntled because of some twisted manly tradition. So what if I asked? I had every right to!

"Calm down, darling." Alexander waved his hand for me to lower my voice. "It's okay. I don't expect anything less from ye."

Sebastian smirked. "It doesn't bother me."

My upper lip twitched, and I had to forcibly stop myself from smiling like a goofy idiot. After our excursion in the park, we were still in a blissful state and it was terribly obvious. I felt the connection between us more intensely, like our bond was getting stronger. I could only imagine how solid it would be after the ceremony.

"I'm very happy for the both of ye," Alexander said with a broad smile. "We'll have the ceremony in Scotland—"

"Say what now?" I interrupted, doing a double take. "Why can't we just do it here where our friends and family are?"

"Yer going to be Queen, Mackenzie. Yer rightful place is in Scotland. It is non-negotiable. Sebastian understands, don't ye boy?"

Bash bowed his head respectfully. "Yes, Alexander."

"Excellent! We'll do a beautiful ceremony in a couple of months when ye return," he said, standing from Bash's chair behind the desk.

"I want a wedding!" I blurted as everyone was moving to leave the room. They all stopped mid-step.

"What?" Bash raised a brow.

"If we're doing it the Lycan way, we'll do it the human way, too. I want a wedding." I crossed my arms over my chest and stomped my foot.

This was absolutely absurd. I never even wanted to get

married before! A poufy white dress sounded like a damn nightmare.

"Mackenzie—" Alexander started, but Bash cut him off.

"Done," he said. "We'll get married the human way, too."

IN ROUGHLY TWENTY-FOUR HOURS, my whole life got twisted upside down and I honestly didn't know how to feel. There also wasn't anyone I could really talk to about it. We agreed to keep the news of our mating a secret for now, but it was killing me not to tell Amy. She already knew I was keeping a secret, and she would respect me and not hound me about it for now. But soon she'd come for me, and there was only so long I could hold out.

Bash woke up early this morning to take Alexander and his guards to Cadwell Estate for a meeting, and I was very curious how that was going to go. Charles was a kiss ass, but at the same time was secretly plotting Alexander's downfall. What a piece of shit. But this meeting provided me the freedom to go to work without any of them breathing down my neck.

I walked into the squad room and everyone was in their respective desks.

"Look who it is," Finn said from across Cas's desk. "Daddy let you out to play?"

"Suck a dick, Finn." I flipped him the middle finger before dropping down at my desk across from Michaels. The others laughed.

"Take it easy, Finn," Cas reprimanded, leaning back in his chair and interlocking his hands behind his head. "It can't be easy being the King's daughter."

"Thank you, Cassidy."

"Oh please, Grey." Finn rolled his eyes. "You're going to be Queen. You *literally* have the world at your fingertips."

"It's not always greener on the other side, Finn," I said solemnly, thinking about all the politics and games that awaited me when I took the crown. I would never be able to rule without looking over my shoulder every day. "Anyway, where are we on the case, Cas?"

Cassidy sat up and pulled out a folder, flipping it open and looking through it. "Well, as you know, the Met was a complete and total bust. Whoever stole the ring, also stole the security footage to cover their tracks, so we're not dealing with an amateur." He flipped through some of the pages until he found what he was looking for. "I know we don't want to believe Maximos's outrageous story about it being the Draupnir, but I followed a hunch and asked a fae friend of mine to look up some history on this elusive ring of Odin's."

"Why fae?" I asked as I bit into the cap of my pen.

"If anyone is going to believe this Norse crap, it'll be them," Cas grunted. "Anyhoo, she confirmed the legend of the Draupnir *and* also told me about other Norse objects related to the ring."

"Like what?" Michaels asked, leaning forward.

Cas looked down at a list of his notes. "Brísingamen, which is a necklace that belonged to the goddess Freyja. Gjöll, the rock to which Fenrir the wolf was bound. And the Skofnung stone, a stone that can heal any wound made by the sword Skofnung."

"This is a joke, right?" I chuckled as I chewed on my pen cap.

"Not in the slightest. At least not to the fae," Cas said as he closed his folder. "Maximos might not be as crazy as we think he is."

I snorted. "Odin isn't real."

"Odin might not be," Finn said. "But they're still legends, and these objects are attached to them. They might be spelled by a witch or warlock and worth a lot."

"Now *that* is a more reasonable hunch. I can get on board with that," I said.

"Regardless," Michaels interrupted, "whoever stole the ring is probably the same person stealing those other objects. We should follow every possible lead."

I nodded. "Agreed. Cas, did your fae friend tell you who those objects belonged to?"

"Yeah, most of them live in the fae realm."

I sighed. "Of course they do. That means we'll need permission to get in. I'll contact our liaison. Get ready to go."

I grabbed my desk phone and checked my phone book for Malakai's number. I dialed and the phone rang a couple times before he answered.

"Hello?"

"Hey, it's Mackenzie."

"Freedom Princess! Long time no chat. I thought the vampires would have eaten you by now," he laughed.

"Funny," I deadpanned. "Can you meet?"

"Yeah, same place as always?"

"Sounds good."

We ended the call and I hurried to grab my things, informing Cas I'd be back in an hour. Instead of meeting in Central Park, Malakai and I had made Battery Park our meeting spot since the Freedom War. The park was at the farthest tip of Manhattan, facing New York Harbor, so it took me a while to get there.

I found our bench and sat there to wait for Malakai, surveying the multitude of people strolling through the park as they walked their dogs or moms walked with their kids in strollers. It was cloudy today, so the heat wasn't so bad.

I didn't have to wait long for Malakai. He plopped himself down after ten minutes. "Freedom Princess," he said by way of greeting. "Or should I call you Curse Breaker now?"

"I hate both names," I grumbled. "Why do people have to put nicknames to people? Mackenzie works just fine."

He chuckled. "You're not just anyone. But you know that, don't you? And that's not why you asked to meet. So why don't you spill why it is you pulled me away from what I was doing?"

I looked at Malakai. He tucked a strand of his shoulder-length chestnut hair behind his ear, exposing the pointy tips. Every time I looked at him, I always got a *Lord of the Rings* vibe.

"I'm working a case and I need access to the fae realm. Can you grant me that?"

He nodded and raised a brow. "I can grant you entrance, but what will you do for me in exchange?"

"Really, Malakai?" I droned. "We're going to negotiate? I thought we were friends!"

"Hardly, Freedom Princess. But let's get close." He scooted toward me.

I scooted away. "What are you talking about?"

"I want a spot on your council," he said. "When you're Queen."

"What?" I exclaimed, darting up from the bench. "You want *that* in exchange for a measly trip to the fae realm? How is that even fair?"

Malakai was insane if he thought I would agree to this absurd deal. I learned my lesson with Bobby Wu. I may have gotten suck-ered once, but never again.

"Because I'm not just giving you access this one time. I'll be granting you infinite access to the fae realm, whenever you like, without a guide or permission. No Lycan other than your father has ever had *that*." Ever since the Freedom War, the fae put restrictions on who could enter the realm.

Well, then. That was definitely a game changer. If I had unlimited access to the fae entrances in New York City and Scot-land, it would make me invaluable. Would I even need access to the fae realm so much? It had been quiet on that front ever since the war, when others in the supernatural community turned their backs on them.

"Trust me, Mackenzie." When he said my name, it snapped me out of my thoughts. "You're going to want access to our realm."

"Why?"

"I can't talk much about it, but things are happening."

His vague answer made my stomach do flips. We couldn't have issues with the fae again. If it was serious, Malakai would tell me. I had to trust it wasn't at this point, that he had it handled.

"Okay, I'll take your deal."

It wasn't a bad idea to have other species in the King's Coun-cil, and with the way things were headed, I needed to seed the Council with people I trusted.

"Perfect." He grinned. "Now tell me ... where do you want your mark?"

Damnit. I was really getting tired of my body getting marked.

WITH A FRESH TATTOO on my shoulder blade in the shape of a fae rune, I now had unlimited access to the fae realm. But just as easily as I got it, it could be removed if I didn't hold up my end of the bargain. He didn't have to tell me it wouldn't be done gently.

The whole exchange took longer than an hour, and I hurriedly texted Cas to meet me in Central Park. Traffic was ridiculous that time of day, and by the time I reached the lake of Central Park, Cas was already waiting for me.

"What took you so long?" he asked as he met me halfway.

"Long story," I said, pushing him back toward the lake. "Come on, let's go."

"Where's Malakai? Don't we need him to enter?"

I shook my head. "Not anymore. I have free access into the realm now."

Cassidy dug in his heels and whirled around me. "Hold up. How the hell did *that* happen?"

I sighed heavily and pulled the neck of my shirt down to show him my back. "A little fae magic. Sort of like the tattoo on my hip."

"What did you give him for it?" Cas asked shrewdly as he brushed his fingers over my skin.

"Don't worry about it." I adjusted my shirt. "Come on, let's stop wasting time." I started toward the lake, not bothering with his protests behind me. I didn't plan to tell Cas about the deal I made with Malakai. That was our business, and our business only.

When we reached the edge of the lake, I placed my hand on top of the water and let it idle there until the surface started to tremble beneath me. In moments, the water parted down the middle and two walls about twenty feet tall on either side of us whooshed into the air. I remembered it from the last time I entered the fae realm with Ranulf. I grabbed Cas's hand and dragged him behind me as I started to walk down the pathway. Once we got to the mid-way point, the water started to close along the trail we'd just left. Up ahead was a wall of water that shimmered before us; I could see the lush green lands of the fae realm through the glistening wall.

"We have to go through it," I instructed Cas. I kept a firm hold on his hand and together, we stepped through the wall of water and were transported into the fae realm.

The sun was burning brightly, and I held up my free hand to cover my eyes and take in the picturesque landscape that made me think I'd walked into a fairy tale. The sky was so blue, the grass so green, and the air so crisp, it just seemed unreal.

"Wow," Cassidy muttered as he took everything in.

"Welcome to the fae realm."

8

"So, where are we going?" I asked as I released his hand.

Cassidy pulled a folded sheet of paper from his back pocket and unfolded it. "We're going into town, and according to Malakai, it's straight through the forest. We just need to follow the path."

Last time I went into these woods, Ranulf and I walked in circles for hours. I was not looking forward to it. The fae realm liked to play a lot of tricks.

As we stepped closer to the entrance to the woods that stood in front of the opening to Central Park, the trees opened to let us through. As soon as we entered, they groaned as they closed behind us. We were enclosed in darkness as the trees covered the sunlight. A clear path zig zagged through the forest and we walked it for a while before I heard a buzzing sound. I tensed and my shoulders hitched up to my ears as I had a PTSD flashback.

"Oh, no," I muttered as I grabbed onto Cas's shirt.

"What's wrong?" He stopped walking.

"Pixies!" I screamed and dropped to the ground, covering my head. Fucking Tinkerbells.

"Singular pixie, thank you very much," a high-pitched voice said into my ear.

I shrieked and fell on my ass, then swatted my hand around my face to get it away from me. "Shoo!"

"I'm here to help you, just so you know, you ungrateful wolf!" she shrilled.

"How are you here to help us?" Cassidy asked as he gave me a hand to help me up.

"Malakai sent me," the pixie sniffed indignantly as she buzzed around us. She looked like a tiny human with transparent wings. It was super weird. "The name's Nyx. I'm here to make sure you don't get lost in the woods."

Malakai sent her? Why wouldn't he tell me? Fuck, if only he knew these little things scared the living crap out of me. I nearly shit a brick.

"Nice to meet you, Nyx," Cas greeted formally, giving me side eye. "Please lead the way."

She crossed her little arms over her chest and stared at me, clearing her throat.

"What?" I said breathlessly.

"Don't you have anything to say to me?" she said, tapping her foot as if she wasn't floating in the air.

"Sorry," I sighed, exasperated. "It's nice to meet you too." I tried very hard not to roll my eyes.

"Good!" She clapped her hands. "Now come and follow me!" She buzzed ahead and we followed. I glared at Cas and he offered a sympathetic look.

We kept on the trail behind Nyx, but for some reason I kept

tripping on lifted tree roots that weren't there when I was looking ahead. On the fifth time, I finally stopped walking, halting our movements.

"What's up?" Cas stopped beside me.

"Do you not see me tripping over myself?"

He chuckled. "Yeah, but I just thought you were clumsy."

"Funny, asshole. How come you're not tripping? The roots are only rising for me."

"What's the hold up?" Nyx called out a couple feet ahead of us. She buzzed back and stopped near my face. A little too close.

"Why are the trees trying to make me fall?" I asked with a knowing look.

"Uh ..." Nyx looked around the forest and blew out a breath, shrugging. "I don't know. What a mystery," she said dryly.

"Right," I deadpanned. "You have no clue," I said sarcastically.

"Maybe you're just not very popular," she said and buzzed away.

Right. I killed their queen. There must be some who still supported her and her rule.

"Don't worry, Kenz. Just watch your step." Cas grabbed my elbow gently and we followed the pixie.

We walked for another fifteen minutes and it was like I was playing a game of hopscotch as I dodged the lifted tree roots at the last minute. I could hear Nyx chuckling up ahead and knew deep down she had something to do with it. In my book, pixies were evil and I didn't trust them.

Nyx flew around and landed on my shoulder, making me practically jump out of my skin.

"What exactly is the purpose of you being here?" I asked, tilting my head to the side.

"To make sure the forest doesn't play any tricks on you," she said as she took a seat on my shoulder.

"You're not doing a very good job at that," I grumbled.

"Oh, don't be such a baby, Queen Slayer. You can't expect everyone to bow at your feet. There are many who loved Drusilla —many who still do—and fae live long lives. They don't forget."

"Did you love Drusilla?" I asked out of curiosity.

"I loved her dearly," Nyx said without skipping a beat. "I was loyal to her until the bitter end."

I was definitely not comfortable with Nyx on my shoulder right at this moment.

"So why are you helping me?"

Nyx flew up and floated in front of my face, grinning. "I have my reasons. We're here."

"Huh?" I said just as the trees parted and we stepped out into the outskirts of a bustling town. I'd been so engrossed in my conversation with the pixie, I didn't realize how much time had passed.

"I will meet you back here in an hour to escort you back through the forest," Nyx said. With that, she flew away without a backwards glance.

THE FAE TOWN reminded me a lot of Sheunta Village. Cobblestone streets, old-fashioned storefronts, and cottages for homes. It seemed like something straight out of a Gothic storybook, complete with pointy ears everywhere. Our round ears made us stand out like a sore thumb. It was painfully obvious we weren't fae, and from Cassidy's size, it was obvious he was Lycan. Relationships between the two species still weren't the best, so we got plenty of looks as we walked the streets. And they weren't all friendly.

"His house is just around this bend," Cas said as he followed the map we'd been given.

We turned the corner and saw a tidy row of cottages. The fae we were looking for lived in the third one down. A white picket fence surrounded the cottage, protecting a small grassy area in the front and a winding stone pathway that led to the front door. I unlatched the fence door and we entered, then walked along the path to the door.

I knocked three times and took a step back to wait for the door to open.

After a moment, the door swung open and an older man with a bald spot at the top of his head appeared. He was hunched over a little, age spots covering his hands, and his hair was the purest shade of white. And of course, he had pointy fae ears.

"Phineas Longsworth?" Cassidy asked.

"Yes?" The older man's voice trembled a little.

"Hello, Mr. Longsworth." Cas flashed his badge. "We're with the Supernatural Investigative Unit, and we're here regarding the theft of a necklace you had in your possession."

Phineas closed the door slightly, leaving just a crack for us to see him and for him to speak through. "Brísingamen, yes, but this is not your jurisdiction. I did not call the SIU."

"We know," I said as I pushed the door wider, making him stumble back as I barged my way inside. "We're following up on a case that happens to coincide with your theft."

"Hey! I did not invite you in!" the old man sputtered.

"We're just here for a friendly chat." I gave him a sweet smile. Cas followed behind me and we walked further into the cottage.

We ambled down a short hallway and I turned into the living room, pleased to see it was empty. Across from the living room was the kitchen, which meant the other doorways in the hallway must lead to bedrooms and bathrooms. It was very important to scope the layout of a place in case of emergencies.

I sat down on the sofa and made myself comfortable just as Phineas hobbled his way over to the living room.

"I don't know what it is you expect me to tell you," he spat, his lower lip trembling as if it were a tick.

"Tell us about this necklace," I suggested. "Why would someone want to steal it?"

"It is Freyja's necklace; nothing special about it. I don't know *why* someone would steal it."

I made the sound of a buzzer. "Wrong! You know why, I can tell. What aren't you telling us, old man?"

"You're better off being truthful, Mr. Longsworth. We can help," Cas advised nicely.

Phineas looked between us and then his aged eyes landed on me. "I knew I recognized you. You're the Queen Slayer, aren't you?"

Shit. "If that's what you want to call me, sure, we'll go with that."

"It's very brave of you to come here, girl," he said, hobbling closer to us. "You are not well-liked in the fae realm."

"I'm not liked anywhere," I complained.

When I really thought about it, it was the truth. The fae didn't like me, the vamps reviled me, and the male Lycans despised me.

It was true – I wasn't popular. Not that I truly cared about that. It was just my laundry list of enemies.

"Does that not bother you, Queen Slayer?" His keen eyes narrowed, observing me.

What was he looking at? I really wished they would stop calling me Queen Slayer. I had enough nicknames as it was.

"I do everything for a reason, Mr. Longsworth, whether it's to free the Lunas or protect my loved ones. But nothing I do is just for kicks. I will always protect those in need, no matter what. So whether people like me doesn't concern me, because I'm not doing it for accolades. I do it because it's the right thing."

"Hm." He scratched his chin and walked toward the kitchen. "Let me get us some tea."

"There's no need!" Cas protested, but the old man disappeared around the corner and we were left alone.

"He's not going to tell us anything," I grumbled, leaning back onto the sofa. "What's up with these items that have all these people spooked? Maximos was the same way when Michaels and I originally met him and tried to help at The Third Eye."

"These items are connected somehow," Cas proposed. "They must be, if someone is collecting them."

"But why, and why are they only giving us half answers?"

Cas shrugged, and just then, Phineas returned with a pewter tray filled with a tea pot and cups. The tray shook in his hands as he tried to carry it on his own. I took it from him and placed it on the coffee table, then Cas and I stood.

"Thank you for the offer, Mr. Longsworth, but we must be going," Cas declined graciously.

"Please stay for tea." Both Cassidy and I looked at the tea pot, then at each other, then at the old man and shook our heads. We knew better than to accept any drink or food from a fae. "Very well." His shoulders slumped.

Phineas walked with us to the door, trailing along behind me. Cas was ahead of us when I suddenly felt a hand slip in my back pocket. I jumped slightly and turned to Phineas. He put his pointer finger to his lips to keep me quiet and I kept walking. Once the door closed, I put my hand in my back pocket and felt the piece of paper he slipped inside. He had written me a note.

BY THE TIME we made it back to the station it was evening and everyone had already left for the day except for the night shift. Cassidy and I stayed behind to write up the day's reports, and when we were done, he offered to take me home.

"Nah, I think I'll stay and do some work I have left from last week and play catch up," I said as I fiddled with some papers on my desk.

"I can stay with you." Cas stopped mid-step and backtracked to my desk. "The squad room will be empty, and I'd prefer not to leave you alone. Bash would have my balls if something happened to you."

I laughed. "I'll be fine, Chang. Go home; I'll be right behind you. I'll even call an Uber if it makes you feel better."

"All right, Grey," he said uneasily. "Text me when you get home."

"Will do!" I called out when he left the squad room.

I waited a good fifteen minutes to make sure he was gone and no one else was coming in to interrupt me before pulling the scrap of paper from my back pocket. Unfolding it, I quickly read what it said.

Meet me tonight at my house. 9pm. Come alone. Do not trust the SIU.

Well, *that* was cryptic. If he didn't trust the SIU, why trust me? I worked for them. Hell, Cas was much nicer to him than I was. He would have been better off slipping the note to him.

I checked my phone and saw it was just past eight P.M. If I was going to meet Phineas, I needed to leave now or I wouldn't make it on time. Before leaving, I shot Bash a quick text to let him know I would be home late.

Grabbing my bag, I hurried out of the SIU and practically ran to Central Park. I was out of breath when I finally entered the park and maneuvered my way past civilians to get to the lake. Too much time had passed, and it took me longer than I thought to get there. Luckily, there was no one near the lake and I could open the fae realm unseen.

I placed my hand on top of the lake and watched breathlessly as the water parted. Wasting no time, I sprinted down the middle until I approached the shimmering wall of water and crashed through it, not bothering to admire its beauty against the moonlight. When I stepped into the fae realm, it was covered in darkness and looked nothing how it had during the daytime. There was an eeriness to it that made a shiver run down my spine. The unearthly hoot of an owl echoed in the far distance and seemed to come from all sides. Instead of continuing to freak myself out, I rushed toward the forest.

My bag thumped against my thigh as I ran down the trail, my breathing heavy and the blood pumping in my ears. I felt the trees watching me, but there was no trickery tonight. They let me through with ease, for which I was grateful. Then again, it could all be part of their game.

When I burst out of the forest and into the outskirts of town, I was struck by how quiet things seemed. Only the flickering glow of streetlamps lit the way. I checked my phone and saw it was five minutes past nine. I was late.

I followed the same path I took with Cas to the street with the row of cottages and stopped at the third house. The lights inside were on. I opened the gate soundlessly and crept along the winding path that led to the front door, then paused when I noticed the front door was slightly ajar.

I pushed it open a little further, making it creak in the stillness. "Phineas?" Nothing but silence. The metallic scent of blood lingered in the air. I pushed the door open enough to squeeze through and went inside, walking silently through the hallway, keeping my senses alert.

The bedroom doors were shut, just like when we were there earlier, so I continued down the hallway and entered the living room. That was when I saw him.

Phineas was lying on top of his crushed coffee table with a hole in his abdomen. Bloodshot eyes were wide open, matching the wide maw of his mouth as if he'd tried to scream. His arms and legs were spread over the table. I didn't know the old man, but he didn't deserve this. Someone was willing to kill him to keep him from sharing whatever it was he wanted to tell me.

I walked toward him with the intention of closing his eyes out of respect, when my feet crunched some glass from the coffee table. I froze in place when I heard a breath hitch. My reflexes were fast, but not fast enough. Someone came soaring out of the kitchen and tackled me to the ground. Before I could react, he vibrated and stretched into two people instead of one.

It was the Gemini. *Fuck.*

One punched me in the face while the other jabbed me in the gut before grabbing me by the hair and dragging me across the room. I roared as I managed a half shift and dug my claws into the carpet. I didn't care about my hair, they could rip it out, for all I cared. The one dragging me by my hair jerked to a stop, and I took that moment to flip around and stand, facing him and clawing him across the throat. He released me and clutched his neck with a startled expression. I kicked my leg back and hit the other one in the gut as he approached from behind, but it wasn't enough.

He vibrated again and turned into three, then four. The Gemini knew better than to use magic because it wouldn't work on me, but they were incredibly strong. If they kept multiplying, there was no way I could take them all on my own.

They came for me at once and I could barely block their blows, much less get a hit in. One hit me in the spine, making me arch my back as a shriek escaped and I collapsed to my knees. Another wrapped an arm around my neck, immobilizing me completely. I wasn't sure what nerve they hit in my spine, but I couldn't move. The one behind me geared up to snap my neck, and all I could think was, *I'm not a vampire. I won't come back to life.*

I took a deep breath and closed my eyes. This was it. I wasn't one to give up, but there was nothing else I could do. I knew when I'd been defeated. I gritted my teeth and hoped Bash could hear my plea. *I love you, Bash*—

In a flash, my whole body spun around and I was dropped on the ground, lying flat on my back. I opened one eye and realized I wasn't dead. *What the hell?* I stared at the ceiling of Phineas's cottage and turned my head to see what was happening, which was when I saw Úlfur fighting the Gemini. I realized he must have ripped my attacker off me, and the force knocked me to the ground.

I couldn't tell what type of supernatural Úlfur was, but he fought with a grace unlike anything I'd ever seen before. With fluid ease, the Gemini couldn't get a single hit on him as he swerved out of their way every single time. He grabbed one and snapped its back, causing all of them to drop to the ground. He must have killed the original Gemini.

Úlfur looked around the room at the mess and his eyes landed on me. "Little wolf." He grinned. "Didn't I tell you to stay out of it?"

"I'm not good at taking orders," I said, trying to wiggle but unable to move. "A little help here?"

"What's wrong with you?" He raised a brow.

"I don't know. They hit me in my spine and now I can't move."

"Ah, no worries." He walked over and dropped to a knee beside me. Úlfur rolled me onto my side with my back facing him, and then he cracked my back.

I let out a blood-curdling scream. "Son of a bitch!" I yelled as my hands gripped the carpet.

"All better." He patted my back. "Now, why don't you tell me what in the bloody hell you were doing here?"

Gasping, I staggered into a sitting position but stayed on the ground. "What do you think? Phineas told me to meet him. When I got here, he was already dead. That damn Gemini must have killed him just before I got here. He didn't get a chance to leave."

"What did I tell you, little wolf—"

"I'm not listening to you!" I shouted, not caring about the neighbors. "Phineas died because he was going to tell me a secret, and I'll make it my mission to find out what he died for. This is *my* case!"

"It's not your time to get involved just yet," he said, stuffing his hands in his pockets.

"What does that even mean? You keep giving me vague responses, and I don't even know who the hell you are. I don't trust you."

Úlfur gave me a mischievous smirk that only made me mistrust him even more. "All the items that have been stolen have been kept separate for a reason, and it's imperative that they stay that way. Someone is trying very hard to put them together."

My brows rose. He was actually giving me information. "Is that what Phineas was going to tell me?"

He nodded.

"What happens if they're put together?" I asked, climbing to my feet.

He tilted his head. "How do I know you won't be tempted if you knew?" His dark eyes drilled into me.

I snorted. "Unless it makes an infinite amount of coffee, I won't be tempted by anything."

"Many humans for centuries have said the same, yet have been lured by the promise of these objects. Words are meaningless."

"Luckily, I'm not human." I crossed my arms over my chest. "Now stop stalling and spill."

Úlfur sighed as if he were tired of me already. "If the objects are melted together, they make a stone, which transforms into a promise from the gods—health, beauty, wealth, power. All your deepest desires ... what many are willing to kill for. With this stone, not only will its gifts be bestowed upon the bearer, but those same gifts will be passed down to future generations of their families as long as the stone stays in their possession. If it's ever taken away, they lose it all in a horrific way."

My eyes narrowed on Úlfur. He couldn't really think I believed that crap. *Did* I believe it? Were there gods? Was this Odin business real? No way. I refused to even consider it. Although ... the book from the archivist about Oracles *did* say Adaline could hear the whispers of the gods. Was that what it meant? Was it referring to *these* gods?

"I can see the wheels spinning in your head, little wolf. What are you thinking?"

I shrugged. "I just don't believe in Odin and all that Norse mythology crap. That's stuff you see in movies. It's not real."

He laughed. "You see werewolves in movies. How come you believe in that?"

"Because I am one," I deadpanned. "Plus, I've never seen Odin."

Úlfur smirked. "You need to broaden your scope, little wolf. You'd be surprised what the world holds."

That was easy for him to say. Either way, the problem remained that people were out there killing and stealing for a legend that may or may not be true. I had no problem being the pessimist in this scenario. People who were willing to kill for the promise of a legend were very dangerous. Well, technically *anyone* who was willing to kill was dangerous, but these people were off their rocker. And so far, they had accumulated two of the objects needed for this so-called ritual. We needed to get to the other two before it was too late.

"So why are you so interested in these objects?" I questioned, eyeing him carefully. He might have given me a lead, but I still didn't trust him. He wasn't as innocent and disinterested as he tried to portray.

"Let's just say I have a special interest in a certain object. That's all you need to know. My goal is to keep them separated, as they should be."

"And just like you said, how do I know you won't be tempted by what those objects can give you?"

He grunted. "Because I'm not human, for one, and two, I have everything I want. Do you see this face?" He pointed to his face. "I don't need beauty. I already have it."

I rolled my eyes. "Smug bastard," I grumbled. "So what are you?"

"That's for me to know and for you to find out when I desire," he smirked. "Since we're done here, let's get out of this dreadful realm. From what I hear, you're not very well-liked around these parts. I'll escort you back to the entrance."

9

It was late by the time I tip-toed into the house. I dropped my bag next to the door and locked it behind me as I crept further inside, just to be stopped by Bash, who was sitting in the darkened living room like a parent. Dressed in only his pajama bottoms, his chest and feet were bare and his right ankle rested on his left knee.

"When you said you'd be home late, I didn't expect you to come home at two in the morning, Mackenzie." He sniffed the air and his blue eyes narrowed. "You smell like blood."

"I've heard it can be an enticing aroma." I bit my lower lip.

"Mackenzie," he glowered.

"If you're a vampire, I guess," I mumbled as I shuffled further into the living room. "Look, I was following up on a lead for a case I'm working on and it took longer than expected. You knew my job would be like this sometimes."

Bash ran a hand through his ink-like hair. "I can't sleep not knowing where you are, not knowing if you're safe or not." He paused and turned to me with a somber expression. "I got a really bad feeling tonight – a heaviness in my gut, and I thought I was going to be sick. I thought something was wrong with you."

My eyes widened slightly as I thought about the moment when the Gemini was about to snap my neck. That was probably when he got the feeling through our bond. If Úlfur hadn't arrived when he did, I would be dead—forcing Bash to go through agonizing pain until his eventual death. I needed to be more careful. I wasn't in charge of just one life anymore, I had to think about Bash, too.

Chastised, I walked over to him and dropped to a knee, resting my hands on his thigh. "I'm perfectly okay, Bash. I'm sorry I worried you, but I—"

"What happened, Mackenzie?" His eyes roamed over my face, searching for an answer.

I gave him a small smile. "I told you, I'm working a case."

"Come here." He pulled me up and sat me next to him on the sofa. As he wrapped his arms around me, I nestled myself in the warmth of his side, bringing my knees to my chest. "Is this case dangerous?"

I rested my head on his chest. "Everything I do is dangerous, Bash."

"Do you have back-up? Do you need me or the Pack?"

I shook my head. "I have the team. Don't worry. Don't stress yourself out, Bash. Everything is okay."

There was a pregnant pause before he said, "You only have six months before you have to leave the SIU. Have you told them?"

"No. I think it's too soon to say anything. They just got me back. I can't tell them just yet."

"You'll be leaving one danger for another," he sighed, running his fingers through my hair. "When will it stop?"

"Do you understand now why I don't want any children?" I lifted my head to face him.

He frowned. "I think I do."

I felt a stinging in my eyes as I watched Bash. I knew it must have taken a lot for him to admit he understood my reasons, because he wanted a family so badly. But my logic was starting to make a lot more sense to him now. The danger would never stop. Not for us, at least.

"There's something we haven't really discussed," I mumbled and sat back, putting some space between us.

"What is it?"

"You're Alpha of the Brooklyn Pack; your place is here. What will happen to us once I leave for Scotland?"

This thought had been nagging in the back of my head since the minute Alexander told me I had six months before taking the throne. It was like an internal clock started ticking and all my concerns rolled out in a lengthy list, topped by this one. I didn't expect him to follow me. I knew how much being Alpha meant to him, and I couldn't ask him to give it up. But a long-distance relationship with a whole ocean between us would be challenging.

"You want to have this conversation now, Mackenzie?" He eyed me.

"Well, when do you want to have it? The day before I leave?" I said sarcastically.

"Don't be a smart ass." He rolled his eyes. "I was just trying to say it's late, and that maybe we could wait until tomorrow when we're rested to talk about this."

My stomach was in knots. "Why would I need rest? You can

just tell me now. The answer will obviously still be the same now or in the morning." I could hear myself getting agitated and defensive. I needed to calm down.

Bash tried to keep from laughing.

"This isn't funny!" I pushed his shoulder, which only made him laugh out loud.

"No matter how tough you act, Mackenzie, you're scared." He caressed my cheek. "I like seeing your vulnerable side. You don't show it often."

How wrong he was. I felt like I had open wounds everywhere for the world to see and throw salt at.

"Mackenzie, don't you understand how much I love you?" he said, those clear blue eyes staring deeply into mine. "I'll go anywhere you go."

"But what about—"

"I plan to give up my position as Alpha."

My jaw dropped. I could catch flies with my open mouth.

"Sebastian!" I gasped. "I can't ask that of you."

"Good thing you're not asking me. This is a decision I made myself. I knew the time would eventually come where I'd have to choose between you and being Alpha, and the choice was painfully clear. There was no doubt in my mind who won that battle."

"You ... you would give up your title, everything ... just to be with me?" I couldn't understand it. Even if we were together, he couldn't be King; he'd be a Prince consort with no real power. If I hadn't freed the Lunas, this might be a very different story.

"I don't care about that, Mackenzie. I've been Alpha for a long time and I'm ready for the next chapter of my life. And that includes you, not the Brooklyn Pack."

I covered my mouth with my hands, clearly surprised. "Charles won't be happy about that. Who will take your place?"

"I'm grooming Jackson," he said as if he'd been planning this for some time. "He is aware the time is coming near."

"What about Amy? Doesn't she have to be a Luna?" A million questions raced through my mind, but I would never forget how V always reminded me how she'd be the Luna's Alpha.

"Yeah, there are some things we need to find workarounds for," Bash chuckled. "But that will all come with time. No need to stress about it now."

I blew out a breath. "Okay. So, we're doing this. All of it. Marriage, mating, moving to Scotland. All the M's."

"Yes we are."

Damn. Have I lost my mind?

A COUPLE DAYS passed without a break on the case. Cas was trying to get in contact with the owners of the two other objects that had been stolen. In the meantime, I had familial obligations. Sebastian lent Ollie his SUV and we were pulling into the driveway of our childhood home in Cold Springs, New York with Alexander sitting in the backseat. It was a comfortable drive, consisting mainly of Alexander telling Ollie about Lycan stuff while I let them talk it out, staying out of it. Mostly because I knew I'd have to engage when I got to my parents' house, and I needed to reserve all my energy for that. This was going to be interesting.

"Okay, Alexander, remember they're totally human. They don't know anything, so don't be weird, and remember they don't know about Ollie, and—"

"Darling," Alexander placed a hand on my shoulder, "I've interacted with humans before. Don worry."

"Relax, sis. Everything's going to be fine." Ollie put an arm around me and grinned. We walked up to the front door and knocked.

After twenty long seconds, my father opened the door. "There you are! Joyce, they're here!" he yelled over his shoulder. "Come in!"

We walked inside our small childhood home that led straight into a living room where my dad's old raggedy recliner was perched, right in front of the TV. The house was warm and welcoming, and I could smell the food all the way from the door. My dad hugged Ollie, then me.

"Dad, I want you to meet my biological father, Alexander MacCoinnich," I introduced the two and Alexander extended a hand with a bright smile. He was dressed in an immaculate suit and it was obvious he was over dressed, but he wanted to make a good impression. "Alexander, this is my father, Thomas Grey."

"It is a pleasure to meet ye, Thomas," Alexander said, and you could hear the absolute joy pouring out of him. He really was excited to meet my parents.

"Likewise." My father shook his hand and gave him a tight smile, unsure about him just yet. "Please, join us in the dining room."

"Thank ye," Alexander said and followed him further into the house.

My father was acting very reserved, so I grabbed Ollie's wrist and gave him a look that said, *Shit! Dad doesn't like him.*

We entered the dining room where my mom was placing

dishes on the table. "Oh!" She seemed startled and ran her hands down her apron, smoothing out the wrinkles.

"Hey, Mom," Ollie greeted as he went over to her and gave her a kiss on the cheek. I followed and gave her a hug.

"Mom, this is Alexander MacCoinnich, my biological father. Alexander, this is my mother, Joyce Grey," I said, introducing the two. My mother looked flushed as she looked over Alexander. *Oh, sweet baby Jesus.*

He gave her a winning smile and I rolled my eyes. "A pleasure." He shook her hand delicately.

"Please have a seat," she said, a little out of breath. "I placed you and Mackenzie together."

"Thank ye," he said in his thick Scottish brogue, to which I thought I heard my mother giggle. *Gross.*

We all took our seats, my parents sitting at each end of the table, me and Alexander on one side, and Ollie seated across from us.

"So, is this your first time in the United States?" my dad asked, beginning the conversation as we all started to build our plates.

"No." Alexander shook his head. "I've been here plenty of times."

"But you're just *now* seeing Mackenzie?" my dad said sharply.

I narrowed my eyes at him. "Dad!"

Alexander tapped his hand on my knee. "It's okay, darling, these questions are to be expected."

"But not right out of the gate," I huffed.

"To answer yer question, Thomas, I didn't know about Mackenzie until not too long ago. When I did, I invited her to stay with me in Scotland, and of course I came to see her here. She is always welcome in Scotland."

I looked down at my plate and avoided my parents' stares. I never told them about Alexander being here during the war. Of course I didn't –we were at war. It wasn't like I could casually let them know and invite him over for dinner back then.

My mother cleared her throat. "How long are you here for?" I peered over at her.

"For as long as Mackenzie will have me." Alexander smiled at me and I smiled back.

"Do you not work?" my dad blurted, and I felt my face get extremely hot.

"Oh my God, Dad," I muttered, wanting to hide under the table. "Stop being so rude."

Alexander took his napkin and dabbed the corners of his mouth before setting it back on his lap. "I'm a multi-millionaire, and I have many businesses. I also have the luxury to take whatever time off I need."

My eyes nearly bugged out of their sockets. *Was he really?* We never really talked about money. Alexander started sending money each month, and at first, I didn't accept. Until I noticed my bank account was slightly larger than I expected. When I checked my statements, I saw multiple deposits from Alexander. He'd been sneaking in small amounts so I wouldn't notice. By then, I just stopped fighting him. He only wanted to help me, even though I was a self-sufficient adult and didn't need his financial support, but whatever. It came in handy when I was put on administrative leave without pay at work.

"Well, isn't *that* nice?" my dad grumbled and started to shovel food into his mouth.

The uncomfortable silence that followed made my skin crawl.

This was not how this dinner was supposed to go. Was my dad jealous? He couldn't be!

Ollie nudged me under the table. I jerked up and glared at him. Then he kicked me hard in the shins. His eyes widened and he nodded at our parents. He was telling me to start a conversation, to smooth things over with them.

Before I could say anything, Alexander cut into the quiet.

"I would just like to say that ye both did a wonderful job raising Mackenzie. I've never met a better human being than her." I felt heat cover my cheeks. "I don believe I would have done a better job. She was with who she was meant to be with. Ye both are her parents."

My mother's eyes glistened and her bottom lip wobbled. She clutched the front of her shirt and smiled at Alexander. "Thank you," she said.

My father's tight grip on his fork loosened, his hand trembling, and he set the fork down and nodded. "That is very kind of you, Alexander," he said. "We love Mackenzie very much."

"I know I can never replace either of ye," Alexander said. "I'm only trying to be a part of her life now, as much as she'll let me. But I know I can never take yer place." He looked specifically at my dad. "I hope ye understand."

The tears started to flow freely for my mom, but they were happy tears. Hearing Alexander's words was a relief for them both. I guessed seeing him in person, especially with how Alexander presented himself with that Alpha aura could be a bit intimidating, and they were hesitant. But now all their fears were put to rest.

The rest of dinner went by smoothly. My parents regaled Alexander with stories of my childhood. From my first soccer game, to when I ran away at the age of eight with only a peanut butter and jelly sandwich, Capri-sun, and my Gameboy, and hid in the treehouse at a neighbor's house. Alexander enjoyed every second of it and I felt a comforting warmth in my gut as I watched him listen to my parents. There was a sense of pure happiness that I hadn't seen in him since we met, and it made him look years younger. But I could also see how much he wished he'd been there, and a part of me wished he was.

After dinner, I offered Alexander a tour of the town so he could see where I grew up. I didn't have to do much to convince him. He picked up his blazer from the back of his chair, which he'd taken off mid-dinner, and shrugged it back on.

"Ma, we'll be back!" I yelled into the kitchen and hurried out with Alexander trailing behind me.

When we stepped outside, I looked to my left and saw my ex-boyfriend James's house. The lights were on and I didn't want his family to see I was home, so I quickly walked down the driveway and onto the sidewalk.

Alexander walked side-by-side with me in silence, and after a couple blocks, he nudged me with his shoulder. "I had a great time, lass." He grinned, his gray eyes sparkling in the night. "Thank ye for the invite."

I smiled. "Anytime. I'm glad you were able to get along with my parents. They mean a lot to me."

He hummed. "I see that. And ye mean a great deal to them. I'm understanding yer human connection much more after today's visit."

"Well, now you know the back story of my childhood," I laughed. "I hope you won't tell anyone about me decapitating my Barbies," I winced.

He chuckled. "Yer secrets are safe with me."

We made it to Main Street and I showed him around, explaining about the Christmas parade the town put on every year and how we helped, and how my mom made biscuits and sausage gravy for the holidays. We were passing Angelina's Pizza when we both tensed.

Alexander grabbed my wrist, halting my steps. "Do ye smell that?" He sniffed the night air.

I did the same and nodded. "Blood." I started toward where the scent was the strongest, but Alexander took the lead and shifted me behind him to shelter me. I wasn't in the mood to argue, especially when there was danger in the area, so I let him. Technically, I should have been protecting him. He was the King, after all.

We inched past a couple of storefronts and turned into an alley, where we saw the body. A human was lying on the ground completely torn up, as if ravaged by an animal.

"This wasn't a wolf," I muttered as I stared at the gashes. "What could have done this?"

"Do ye have animals in this area? It could have been an actual animal attack," he said. "Not everything is supernatural."

He was right. I was so paranoid now, looking for a supernatural problem to everything, that I never stopped to question if maybe, just maybe, this could be a human atrocity.

"I guess I should call the police, then," I said as I went to pull out my cell phone. I turned away from the body when I saw a figure at the entrance of the alley.

Their fingers started to glow and spark this yellowish-gold color at the tips, which morphed into a ball a split second before they launched it toward Alexander's back. Without thinking, I jumped in front of it. "Watch out!" I yelled as I absorbed the force of the magic burst. I was able to repel the magic ball, but the energy knocked me into Alexander.

"Lass! Are ye okay?" I rolled off him and he quickly sat up and checked on me.

I rubbed my chest where the magic hit and grimaced. "Yeah, I'm good. I have a tattoo that stops harmful magic, but that doesn't mean I don't feel the brunt of it sometimes when it's super powerful."

He looked up at the figure and morphed into a half shift in the span of a blink. His eyes glowed silver and his canines slipped out with a growl that roared into the otherwise silent night. Alexander launched, his claws scrabbling on the asphalt, and went into full-on attack mode, effortlessly swerving the magic spheres that were lobbed his way. His speed was beyond supernatural, almost like vampire speed. I'd never seen anything like it. This was why he was Alpha – because he was an unstoppable force. He reached the figure and they sailed into hand-to-hand combat, while I just laid on the ground like a dazed idiot.

I finally stood and sprinted toward them, but honestly, it didn't look like Alexander needed my help. When I got closer, I saw our assailant was a guy, and Alexander was clawing at him, making him bleed out. The man was slowing down and I couldn't tell if he was a warlock or fae. When his fingers sparkled again and he reached for Alex, I snatched his hand and twisted it back in an unnatural way. He screamed.

"That's a no-no." I shook my head and tsked. "No magic. Let's play fair. Now tell us why you attacked and if you were the one who killed that human." With magic, he could have easily killed the human and made it look like an animal attack. "I don't hear any talking," I taunted as I twisted his hand further.

He screamed again and I worried we'd draw attention. "You won't get anything out of me, Curse Breaker," the man snarled.

Alexander's clawed hand went for his neck and he dug his claws in, puncturing skin. "Answer her questions or I'll rip out yer throat," he growled.

"Okay! Okay!" he gurgled as blood seeped out of his mouth. "I killed the human ... to lure you out!" he grunted.

"Why?" I asked, tightening my grip on him.

"There's a bounty on your head in the black market. I didn't know you were immune to magic."

I laughed. Of course there was a bounty on my head, because I couldn't just live a normal life. Someone always had to want me dead. It would be abnormal if they didn't.

"Why aim for Alexander instead of me, then?"

"Everyone knows you protect those you love," he said, defeated. "If you let me live, I won't bother you and I'll give you a piece of vital information."

I snorted. "You'll tell me regardless. Spill."

He grimaced. "The person who set up the bounty is human."

My eyes widened. *Well, then, that's new.* I didn't think I could be shocked until now. I didn't think I'd pissed off any humans lately, but maybe I had.

"Rip out his throat, Alexander." I turned around just as I heard the man's screams cut out.

10

I looked down at the two bodies on the ground and sighed. This was going to be a pain to clean up. The nearest SIU team was back in the city, and by the time they got here, I was sure we would have garnered some human attention. Which meant we had to bury the bodies ourselves. I texted Ollie for some help.

"This is nae good, darling," Alexander said as he went through the pockets of our killer. "Yer nae safe in America."

I snorted. "I'm not safe anywhere. At least here I can figure out who's trying to kill me."

Alexander frowned as he dug through the man's back pocket. "I think I found something."

I squatted on the other side of the body and waited for him to retrieve it. He pulled out a cell phone. A flip phone, at that. Super old school.

"That could be a burner," I suggested as Alexander handed it over to me. I opened it up and looked at the call history. There was only one phone number listed. "I think this is where he communicated with our mystery human."

"Let's call them." Alexander nodded toward the phone.

I shook my head. "Not yet. We'll spook whoever it is. I'll send the number to the SIU and have them do a trace so we can get a general location of where that number is. Then when we call, we do another trace and get an exact location."

Just then, Ollie turned the corner and slipped into the alley. "Holy shit," he mumbled, jerking to a stop at the gruesome sight. "What the hell happened?"

I sighed. "We were attacked by *this* guy," I pointed to the killer, "who killed *that* guy," I jabbed my thumb at the other body, "because he was really after *me*. It's a whole ordeal."

"Do we call the police?" He frowned, looking confused. "You're sort of the police."

I chuckled. "They're busy, so we need to bury the bodies. Did you bring the SUV and shovels?"

He nodded.

"Good. Let's start loading them up!"

BY THE TIME we made it back to Brooklyn, we were beyond exhausted. Disposing of bodies was hard work. When we returned to my parents' house, we had to compel them to forget what they saw since we were covered in blood and dirt. I hated doing that to them, but it was a necessary evil.

"So let me get this straight," Bash started. "You buried their bodies in the woods, where their bodies can be unearthed by animals and found by humans?"

My brows furrowed. "Well, I didn't think about it like that. But now that you mention it, maybe we *should* contact the SIU ..."

"You think?" Bash deadpanned.

"Listen, we were under duress. Did you not hear the part where a *human* put a bounty out on my head? A human!"

Bash laid on our bed and crossed his ankles, resting his hands on his stomach. "Yes, I heard you, Mackenzie."

"Doesn't that concern you? It concerns me. I don't mind having supernatural enemies, but a human? What the hell did I do to them?"

"Humans don't scare me. I'm almost positive the ones behind this are the vampires," Bash said almost certainly.

"I don't know, Bash ..."

He shrugged. "Don't be so quick to believe this man. He was on death's door. He was probably spouting nonsense to save his own ass."

I grinned. "I love it when you curse."

"Mackenzie, stay on track."

"Sorry," I winced. "Anyway, tomorrow I'll give the phone to Finn to trace when I go to work. Let's see what we can get out of it."

I finished drying my hair with a towel and threw on a t-shirt and some underwear and climbed into bed. I was completely drained after the day I had.

Bash turned on his side to face me. "Don't think I'm not worried, Mackenzie, because I am. I worry about you every day." He brushed a damp strand of hair away from my face.

"You know I worry about you too," I murmured.

He quirked a brow. "Really? And why is that?"

"I have so many enemies. You're an easy target."

He grinned. "I can't be captured that easily."

I gave him a sly smile before I pounced, pushing him on his back and straddling him. I took his wrists and held them above his head. "I find it pretty easy," I whispered.

He growled playfully before grabbing me around the waist and flipping me on my back as if I hadn't just been pinning him down. "Only because I let you," he taunted. I couldn't help but laugh.

Bash brushed his finger over my lips. "Quiet, Mackenzie. Your father is just down the hall."

I sighed. I forgot about Alexander. We didn't want to get caught—again. And with wolves' sensitive hearing, it would be way too apparent what we were up to. Damn wolf hearing.

I frowned playfully. "Fine, no play time. Just one little kiss."

THE GANG WAS ALREADY THERE when I walked into SIU headquarters and headed straight to Finn's desk, hopping on top of it and handing him the flip phone.

"This is what we found on the killer," I said, having called him last night and explained what happened.

He took it from me and started to dig in his drawers for a cable to plug it into his computer. "It shouldn't take long," he said as he found the cable and began to set everything up.

Cassidy walked over and I filled him in on what happened. "Do you think it might have something to do with the case?" he asked.

I twisted my mouth to the side as I thought about it. No, it couldn't have anything to do with ... Wait a minute. When I was talking to Úlfur, we both said we couldn't fall for the allure of the objects because we weren't human. I said it just to be a smart ass, but when Úlfur said it, he confirmed supernaturals were stronger and could fight the pull of the objects. So that meant our most likely suspect for the case was human.

"Cas, you're a genius!" I hopped off the desk. "Our suspect is human!"

He tilted his head. "How do you know that?"

Shit, how can I explain this without telling him about Úlfur? "Uh ... Phineas mentioned that supernaturals couldn't fall for the attraction of the objects, unlike humans," I lied. "He told me when we were walking out of his house."

"Well, that's good to know." Cas nodded. "But it also broadens our scope and makes it harder to find our culprit."

"Hey, Michaels?" Finn called out. "Help me with this trace. I'll give you the number."

"Go ahead," Michaels said, and Finn rattled off the number.

"We have a registry of humans who are aware of the supernatural community. We can start there," Cas suggested. "The suspect must know about us if they hired a Gemini to do their dirty work."

"Yeah, that sounds good. We can compile a list of suspects from there and see if Maximos knows any of them—"

"End the trace!" Finn shouted as he shot up from his chair, knocking it back in his haste. "Now!"

Cas and I jumped and turned to Michaels, who was scrambling at his computer trying to shut it off.

"Unplug everything!" Finn yelled. He started to unplug his computer and Michaels followed suit while Cas and I stood idly by, not comprehending what just happened. After they were done, Finn was breathing heavily and running a hand through his hair.

"Dude, what happened?" I asked once the quiet got to be too much.

"I didn't finish the trace," Michaels complained. "It was almost complete—"

"I got a general location," Finn muttered, avoiding eye contact. "We may have a problem."

I looked at each of them, but Michaels and Cas appeared just as confused as I was. "Finn, what's wrong?"

He shook his head. "Not here. It's not safe. Conference room. I'll unplug the cameras."

We all tried to inconspicuously meander to the conference room as Finn unplugged the cameras. Michaels closed the blinds for privacy and we stood around the table waiting for Finn to finish.

When all the monitoring devices had been unplugged, he locked the door. I'd never seen Finn so nervous. He was never nervous. He was the most self-assured person I'd ever met. It was almost annoying.

"The number your killer called came from 1PP," Finn finally said.

My eyes bugged out. "What?" Everyone froze.

1PP was One Police Plaza, the human police headquarters, and where I originally interned for Michaels.

"That can't be right," Michaels sputtered, looking at the three of us. "A cop wouldn't—"

"Are you sure about that?" Cas raised a brow. "Humans are known to do a lot of shady things."

Cassidy was right. If the call was to someone from 1PP, they were human. The SIU building was nowhere near the human police headquarters, which meant the guy we killed wasn't lying —the hit order came from a human.

"We had to shut everything down, but if they're smart, they already figured out we traced their number," Finn said. "This is fucked up."

He could say that again. What kind of mess did I get myself into this time, and how? I took a seat in the nearest chair and slumped down, completely drained.

"We need to tell Briggs," Cas suggested. "He needs to know what's going on."

"Can we trust him?" Finn countered. I was surprised he didn't trust Briggs.

"Of course we can trust him," Michaels scoffed. "He had Grey's back when she needed him most."

"This is different," Finn argued, placing his hands on his hips. "We know the SIU is corrupt—"

"Not Briggs," I interrupted. "It's higher up than him."

"If someone in the force is after you, they have the resources. You aren't safe, Grey," Michaels said tightly. Quiet encompassed the room; no one tried to refute his claim.

The truth was obvious: I was royally fucked. A human with the police force in his pocket and supernatural connections was a powerful combination.

"Cas," I turned to the Lycan, "go get Briggs. We'll tell him everything."

He nodded and left the conference room, leaving me alone with Finn and Michaels. I knew I should call Bash and tell him what was going on, but this wasn't something I could convey over the phone. My phone could already be tapped. I didn't know how far this person was willing to take their resources. If they were listening in on my conversations, nothing I said over the phone was safe.

"You can't travel alone," Finn said. "I'll take you home today."

I wanted to roll my eyes and tell him I was fine on my own, that I could handle myself — and I could — but something nagged me. What if I got arrested by the human police again and I was alone? No one would know, and they could deny me my one phone call. There were too many unknown variables and I didn't want to risk it. I decided to accept his help and not be stubborn, for once.

I nodded.

Cas walked in with Briggs behind him. When Cas locked the door behind them, Briggs raised a brow in confusion.

"What the hell is going on here?" he grumbled.

"There's a bounty on my head," I started. "I caught someone trying to kill me when I went home this weekend, and then I found a burner phone in their pocket."

"It had one number in it," Finn picked up the story, "containing the number of the person who we assume put the hit out on Grey."

Briggs looked between us. "Okay, and?"

"We traced the number, boss," Finn said. "It came from IPP."

"Son of a bitch!" Briggs shouted, slamming a fist on the conference table. His face turned beet red and a vein popped on his forehead as he clenched his jaw.

"So, I take it this isn't a surprise?" Michaels asked as he stuffed his hands in his pockets.

"You've made a lot of people angry, Grey," Briggs gritted through his teeth. "Including the Police Commissioner."

"Billie Cardona?" Cas gasped. "*That's* who put the hit out? Why?"

Briggs shook his head. "I'm not a hundred percent sure it's him, but he was furious after your father called to request your reinstatement to the force. He'll know you traced him to IPP."

"I'll lay low." I stood from the chair. "Cas can handle the case on his own. We have somewhat of a lead that I can work on from home."

Briggs nodded and stomped out of the conference room, slamming the door behind him so hard, the windows trembled from the force. It made the rest of us jump and we could only stare at one another, speechless. We dispersed shortly after. Cas handed over the registry that contained the list of humans aware of the supernatural community, and I placed it in my messenger bag to look through when I got home.

"Come on, Grey, I'll take you home," Finn said as he waited for me by the door.

"See you guys later." I waved to Cas and Michaels and followed the Reaper out of the station.

The heat wave blanketing New York City was starting to release its grip and my body temperature was finally beginning to regulate. It was still sweltering, though.

We walked to the train station and hopped on the L train to catch a transfer to Brooklyn Heights, where the Brooklyn Pack resided and where I now lived with Bash. Our home wasn't too far from the Pack's former warehouse in Dumbo, and it was definitely an upgrade.

"You know, you didn't have to walk me home." I smiled sweetly at Finn as we stood and held onto the anchored pole to keep from falling as it swayed and clattered. The train was practically empty, but I wasn't in the mood to sit down.

"I'm going in the same direction. It's no big deal."

"Right." I rolled my eyes. "Well, no one would be stupid enough to attack me on Pack land, so I should be safe at home. I'll stay in the Compound instead of the house, just to be sure."

Finn peered over at me. "You're taking all of this relatively well. I expected some fight from you."

I scoffed. "I do have *some* self-preservation, you know."

"Yeah, but you usually think you can take on the world by yourself."

The train jerked and screeched to a stop. The doors opened and a stream of people entered our train car, while others exited.

"I'm not the same person I was when I was twenty-two. Things have changed." I looked down at my sneaker-clad feet. A lot had happened to force me to grow up since I met Bash and Jonah.

The train started with a lurch and we approached a tunnel, where the lights flickered off and everything went black, which was normal. At least it would have been, until someone wrapped an arm around my neck and yanked me back.

"Shit!" I yelled, releasing my hold on the pole unconsciously.

"Grey!" Finn shouted in the darkness, and I heard a bunch of shuffling in his direction.

I jabbed my elbow into the gut of whomever grabbed me, eliciting a pained grunt, but they kept their hold painfully tight. Someone else grabbed my legs and lifted me up and I started to flail in their grip. I switched on my night vision and scanned my surroundings. Finn was fighting four men, and two others were trying to capture me.

A roar ripped out of me as I morphed into a half-shift. I reached my clawed hands overhead to the one holding my upper body and dug my claws into their face, hoping I could puncture an eye. When they shrieked and released me I collapsed to the ground, my head bouncing on the train floor. I blinked a couple of times, trying to clear the fuzziness. The one holding my legs started dragging me, but I dug my claws into the floor. As he dragged me, I scraped and gouged the floor, leaving claw marks in our wake. My hand finally latched onto a pole and I didn't let go.

"You stupid bitch!" the man snarled as he was yanked to a stop. He released me for just a moment, only to pull me up with the intention of tossing me over his shoulders, but that was the reprieve I needed.

I did a back flip and managed a roundhouse kick to his face. His neck snapped to the side, breaking from the force. I thought I'd gotten him good, but then he adjusted his head and snapped it back in place. He faced me, looking angrier than ever.

"Fuck," I muttered, completely out of breath.

The train continued in motion, but the lights flickered back on and I could see their faces more clearly. I looked over at Finn and noticed the fangs on his attackers. Vampires.

Normally, when I snapped a vampire's neck, it knocked them out for a little while, at least. What the hell were they?

"Come with us," the one in front of me growled.

"Who are you?" My eyes ping-ponged between all of them. If Finn wasn't careful, they'd overpower him.

In response, the guy charged and tackled me to the ground like a linebacker. I slid across the grimy train floor, landing all the way on the other end, away from Finn. The guy who tackled me was a burly man with a military-style buzz cut.

He prowled toward me and I scrambled to my feet, crouching in a fighting stance. When he got close enough, I didn't wait for him to make the first move. I jabbed him in the side and gut, and when he crouched forward, I chopped him on his throat, making him choke. I twirled around behind him, kicking him behind the knee and making him fall to one knee. I ripped my belt off in a flash, unstitching my belt loops from my jeans from the force, and wrapped the leather around his neck, tightening my hold.

"Tell me who sent you!" I growled in his ear. "Or else your head's coming off."

"I'm not telling you shit," he choked out as he scrabbled to release the belt from his neck.

I tightened it, turning around so we were back-to-back, and pulled the belt straps over my shoulder with as much force as I could muster. Over my gritted yell, I heard the pop of his neck and the ripping of his skin. Then I was propelled forward as his head released from his body and rolled down the floor. His body collapsed with a trembling thud.

I clambered to my feet just as another assailant headed my way, but the train was slowing down and I knew we were coming to a stop. This was their opportunity to snatch me up, especially if they had someone waiting at this stop.

Finn was thinking the same thing, because he suddenly dissolved before their eyes just as one of them tried to grab him, becoming a wispy cloud of black smoke. Finn swirled toward me and engulfed me completely. I lost all sense of touch and sight, but I could tell I was no longer on my feet. I was weightless, floating within the cloud that was Finn. I didn't know if we were moving or not, but I twirled around and stayed calm. I had to trust Finn. The smoke didn't feel hot or cold; it didn't have a feeling at all, other than being strange.

After a while I started to get nervous. "Finn? Hello? Say something!" Silence. It went on for some time, and then, just as I was about to start panicking, I touched solid ground and the black cloud wafted around me to in front of me and materialized into Finn.

I was startled to realize we were in front of my brownstone house. "How did we get here?" I asked, completely perplexed.

"I flew us here. It wasn't safe to travel by foot—"

"What do you mean you *flew* here? Wouldn't it have been obvious that I was floating in the sky?"

He shrugged. "I turned you into a cloud of smoke with me."

My jaw dropped. "You can do that?"

He nodded.

"Who were those guys on the train?" I asked, shaking my head as I shook out the idea that I'd been a cloud of smoke.

Finn scanned the streets warily. "They were vampires for sure, and they asked me for the Gjöll, one of the objects."

"That's ..." I squinted as I tried to remember the objects, rubbing my forehead. "I think that's Fenrir's rock, the one he was bound to. Supposedly, he's a wolf in Norse mythology."

"They were after the object and you. That wasn't a coincidence."

"Don't remind me," I snorted. "Tomorrow, go pay a visit to Alistair, the Head Vampire of New York City, and ask him about those vamps that attacked us. He must know something. They don't step out of line as a general rule, which means he gave them permission."

Finn nodded. "Will do. Now get inside. It's not safe to be out in the open."

I patted him on the upper arm. "Thanks for having my back."

"Always, Grey."

We parted ways and I trudged up the steps to the front door, opening it up and locking it behind me. I dropped my bag beside the door like always and aimed straight for the kitchen. I'd put a hold on coffee because it was too hot outside and it seemed like the perfect time to cut back on my addiction, but right now, I needed my crack.

Grabbing the bag of coffee grounds, I started the coffee maker and the smell of java engulfed the house in seconds. I opened the cabinet where the mugs were located, picked my favorite one, and started to prepare it—two sugars, light milk. I hated flavored creamers.

"What's going on here?" Bash said from the kitchen entryway.

My nerves were frayed and I jumped because I didn't hear him approach. "Just making some coffee," I mumbled.

"I thought you were cutting back?"

"And I have, but today was rough. I need this." I turned around to face him. He could read it all in my expression.

"What happened?"

I told him everything. What we found in the cellphone, what the trace revealed, who our suspect was, and what happened on the train. He listened carefully without interrupting as I word vomited it all.

"I'm going to lay low, and it's probably a good idea to stay at the Compound, right?" He raised a brow. "What?"

"I'm surprised you're suggesting it, that's all. I thought being sequestered would be the last thing you'd want," he said as he came around the kitchen island.

"Well, when you say it like that, you make me not want to do it," I sighed. I turned back to the coffee pot and poured the elixir of life into my mug, stirring it and taking a much-needed sip.

"You know what I'm going to say, right?" Bash quirked a brow.

I blew a breath. "I know we got this bond and all, but I'm still not a mind reader, babe. What is it you're going to say?"

He smirked. "You're not leaving my side for the foreseeable future."

I frowned. "You know what? I really should have known you'd say that. You're such a damn Alpha." I took a big gulp of my coffee before setting it down on the counter. "Look, I'm not going to be attached at the hip with you. I don't need a personal bodyguard, okay, Kevin Costner?"

"This is all going in one ear and out the other." He shrugged and started to walk out of the kitchen.

"Ugh! You stubborn wolf!" I yelled at his retreating figure.

I wanted to be around the Pack, sure, but I didn't want a shadow. And Bash could be a little extra with his protectiveness. This was a recipe for disaster. Unfortunately, if I wanted to survive this without any hiccups, I had to follow suit. *Damnit.*

I finished my coffee and rinsed out my mug, and just as I was about to turn off the lights and head upstairs, Alexander walked in, Ranulf trailing behind him.

"Hold yer horses, lass." Alexander held up a hand to stop me from walking out and pushed me back into the kitchen. "I spoke to Sebastian." Of course he did.

"I have it all under control," I said quickly. "No need to worry."

"Why don ye consider coming to Scotland early, Princess?" Ranulf suggested. "It's much safer."

How could I explain this without sounding like an emotional idiot? I knew they wanted me in Sheunta Village as soon as possible because it was safest, but there was still so much for me to do before I was forced to move there, and I couldn't leave without cleaning up the messes I'd made.

"It's not time. Not yet."

"Soon, ye won't have the option, darling," Alexander said kindly.

"I understand that, and I know my timeline, but I still have work to do. This current problem will get resolved. It's just a little hiccup." I grimaced as I said it. How many hiccups could a person really have?

"If ye insist," Alexander said, unconvinced. "But Ranulf will be by yer side until this is resolved."

I laughed bitterly. If I didn't allow Bash to follow me, Alexander would assign someone to do the job. I was surrounded by overbearing men. When would it be *my* turn?

I grinned wickedly. "Sure, Ranulf can be my babysitter again."

He growled. "I was never yer babysitter, ye stupid girl."

"Sure you weren't." I winked at him. It only pissed him off further, which made me laugh.

We agreed I could stay at the house instead of going to the Compound as long as Ranulf was with me, and Alexander headed to his room, leaving me with Ranulf to sit in the living room with me as I watched TV and flipped through the human registry. This would be terribly boring for him.

I made myself comfortable on the sofa and opened the book that listed all the humans who were aware of the supernatural community. There were numerous politicians in there, which I shouldn't have been surprised about, peppered with the occasional celebrity, but mostly it was random people I'd never heard of before. Deducing who our mystery string-puller was would be difficult. Unfortunately, the registry wasn't organized in any kind of specific order, so I had to go through the whole thing just to jot down the ones located in New York City. And even then, it was a long shot. A human could have traveled to New York from another location for these objects. That just made this much harder.

11

I'd fallen asleep on the sofa, my face plastered to the pages of the book, stuck to the paper with drool. I lifted my head and peered around the room, seeing early morning light shining through the living room window. Ranulf was asleep on the armchair, his head thrown back and mouth wide open, little snores gurgling out. I had to cover my mouth and swallow a laugh.

The house was quiet. There was no movement upstairs and no one was in the kitchen, so I assumed Bash and Ollie were at the Compound. I was about to wake up Ranulf when my phone buzzed.

I pulled it out of my pocket and looked at the screen. I didn't recognize the number, but I answered anyway. "Hello?" I whispered.

"Mackenzie Grey, how lovely to hear your voice," a man said through the line.

"Who is this?" I said more sternly, creeping to the edge of the sofa.

"Who you've been looking for. Let's not play coy; I know you traced my number."

"Commissioner Cardona," I breathed.

He chuckled. "So you're not just a pretty face. I think it's time we meet, Mackenzie. Sixty-ninth street transfer bridge. Come alone." Before I could respond, the call disconnected.

I looked at my phone screen and then at Ranulf, who was still asleep. I could wake him for back-up or go on my own. But if I showed up with Ranulf, Cardona may not show himself. I couldn't take the risk. Decision made, I quietly stood and tiptoed out of the room, going to my bag by the door to grab my wallet and snatch my ID, metro card, and some cash. Less than five minutes after the phone call, I was out the door and sprinting to the nearest subway station.

Why Cardona wanted to meet at the bridge was beyond me, unless he hoped to dump my lifeless body in the Hudson River. The bridge was under renovation, but there would most likely still be people milling about. Unless he wanted to meet somewhere more public, in which case, Penn station would have been better. But who was I to tell him how to be a better villain?

After a short train ride into the city and a couple of bus transfers, I finally made it to my meeting spot with the Commissioner. No one was around—as expected. The area was closed off since it was being renovated, but I ducked past the barriers and went to stand by the bridge.

The minutes ticked by and I kept looking at my watch, but once I reached the thirty-minute mark, I decided this was a wash. As I turned to leave, a blacked-out SUV drove up to the barrier.

After parking as close as the car could get, multiple doors opened. I saw Billie Cardona exit from the back, flanked by two hulking men as they walked toward me.

"Mackenzie Grey." He smiled broadly, his arms outstretched. "You came."

Police Commissioner Billie Cardona was a human in his fifties who looked older than he was. The years hadn't been kind to him. I didn't have to know him to know he wasn't a good person. His stare was dark and impenetrable, with a glint in his black-hearted eyes that spoke of many evil deeds, even for a human.

"I knew you didn't like me, but to hate me so much you'd put a hit out on me? Wow, that's some serious hatred." I blew out a breath.

He adjusted his expensive tie and craned his neck. "Honestly, Mackenzie, it's true I don't much care for you, but what I want is the Gjöll, and you're in my way."

Talk about a plot twist! *He* was the one collecting the objects? But Maximos was his friend, or his acquaintance—whatever.

"I don't have it," I shrugged, "and I don't know what taking me out will accomplish."

"I know you're close to getting it since you now have free reign in the fae realm. Plus, you're a nuisance. Frankly, I'd be doing the world a favor."

"Why do you want the objects?" I thought about what they offered—wealth, beauty, health, power. What was so special about that?

"It will give me ultimate power!" he growled, taking a step toward me with a wild gleam in his eye. "I would finally be on par with your kind."

Oh. He wanted to be one of us, just without the freakiness that came with being supernatural. Talk about picky.

I sighed and my gaze traveled to his two colossal bodyguards, wondering if they were human or not. This was too much work, and I wasn't in the mood to fight or get my ass kicked right now. Humans needed to learn to stay in their lane.

"You know I can't let you have these objects. Not that I even believe in this legend, but whatever."

Cardona smirked. "I'd like to see you try to stop me."

The two guys that flanked him, looking like beefed-up juice monkeys, stepped toward me threateningly and I cursed.

"Bring it, beef cake." I waved them forward.

One of them ran toward me and I was able to sidestep him in time, but the other bodyguard was a warlock and I didn't see his magic ball aimed for my back until it was too late. I didn't feel the effects of it, thanks to my tattoo, but the force of the blast slammed into me and I knocked the other guy down as I fell.

"Son of a bitch," I muttered as I rolled off him. "Magic does nothing to me, FYI," I tossed over my shoulder.

"But I can still knock you off your feet the good old-fashioned way," the beefcake beside me taunted with a grin. *Damnit.*

When a fist came flying and hit me square in the cheek, I felt my face jiggle in slow motion like Jell-O as my head snapped to the other side. It would have been funny if it didn't hurt like a bitch. I stumbled back and blocked his next hit. Transforming into a half shift, I dug my clawed hand into his gut, feeling his insides and ripping them out. He collapsed to the ground without a whimper.

I licked my canines, my wolf enjoying the smell of fresh blood, and faced off against the warlock. He heaved one magic ball after another, landing on my shoulders with precision. The force made me slide back, losing valuable ground, and I snarled as the bloodlust began to consume me. I refused to let Billie or his beefcake warlock get away.

I strolled toward the warlock, seeing Cardona hauling ass to the SUV from the corner of my eye. *Damnit.* I ran after him, but the warlock stopped me by tackling me to the ground. I elbowed him and kicked him in the groin, which made him roll over and howl in pain. I had a single-minded desire to get to Cardona, but the squealing of tires alerted me that he'd gotten away.

I quickly stood and turned my ire toward the warlock left behind by the Commissioner. "Where did he go?" I growled.

He grunted, "He left me to finish the job." The warlock released a whip of magic that wrapped around me, trapping my arms and legs.

"Shit," I grumbled. I might have been immune to harmful magic, but they could still get creative with it.

He strolled over to me and pulled a dagger from the holster on his hip, bringing it to my neck. "Tell me where the Gjöll is, and I'll make this quick and painless." He pressed the knife to my skin, and I felt a pinch and the trickle of blood.

Cassidy was the one with the list of owners of the objects; I didn't have a clue. They went after the wrong SIU detective. It was almost laughable, but I wasn't going to bait him. If I did that, I would just end up pointing them to Cassidy and I wouldn't do that.

"How can you work for a human?" *Well, maybe I'll bait him just a little.* "He's only using you to get what he wants. But what do you get? You're a freakin' warlock! You're better than this."

He smirked. "You have no idea what I'm getting out of this,

and it's none of your business anyway. Now tell me where it is!" The dagger pressed further into my skin and I tried to pull back.

"She doesn't know," a voice said from behind him, and the warlock whipped around to face our intruder. It was Úlfur. He stood on the now defunct bridge in well-pressed slacks and a crisp, button-up shirt, his dark features giving him a mischievous look. "How many times must I save you, little wolf?"

I tried to shrug, but my magical restraints were too tight. "I don't know, but why don't you help a sista out?"

Úlfur sighed. "Very well." He hopped off the bridge, which was relatively high, and landed easily on the ground. He met the warlock halfway, dodging every magical blast with his unnatural speed and reflexes. With no more effort than he would use if reaching for the remote control, he grabbed the warlock's neck and snapped it. Úlfur tossed the body on the ground and it landed like a lump of coal. The whip of magic dissolved and I could finally move again.

"What the hell are you?" I asked him for what felt like the hundredth time.

He grinned. "Ah, the mysteries of the world. Shouldn't I get a thank you, little wolf?"

I rolled my eyes. "Stop calling me little wolf. I'm not little!"

"But you are, dear Mackenzie. You're a very little thing. One I'm always saving, against my very nature. Why is that?" His eyes narrowed as he studied me.

"I don't know why you do the things you do. You're fuckin' weird, man." I rubbed at my upper arms where I still felt the tightness of the magic rope.

"And you're not worried that my nature is to actually kill

you?" He grinned as if we were playing a game. Maybe to him, we were.

"I'm no stranger to others wanting to kill me—"

"But I'm not like the others. I actually can."

A chill skittered down my spine. His words were icy, spoken with enough conviction that I believed him.

Úlfur watched me as if enjoying my reaction, and I realized I hadn't schooled my expression. It was probably written all over my face, giving him a front row seat to how I felt. I needed to get it together.

I cleared my throat. "Well, since you don't want to kill me right now, why don't we work together?"

"You trust me?" he smirked.

"Fuck no," I blurted. "But we want the same thing. We want the objects separated and out of human hands. Let's make it happen."

"Very well." He nodded. "What do you propose?" He motioned for us to walk and we started to exit the bridge area.

"I learned the human after the objects is Police Commissioner Billie Cardona—"

Úlfur snorted and let out a chuckle.

"Something funny?" I asked.

He waved me off. "No, sorry, continue."

I gave him a weird look but continued my spiel. "He's most likely the one pulling the strings over at the SIU, which means he has a lot of power, and I want to know how. No human should be able to corrupt the SIU; it's just not possible. And with the objects, he'll be more powerful than ever. We can't let that happen."

"Agreed." Úlfur nodded.

"He's looking for the Gjöll. My partner at the SIU knows who the owner is, but—"

"That won't be necessary. I'm in possession of the rock. Next object?"

Surprised, I peered over at him, but continued. "The Skofnung stone—the one that brings health."

"Hm. Does your partner know who owns that one?" Úlfur asked as we walked side-by-side on the sidewalk.

"I believe so. I'll have to ask him when—"

"You cannot let anyone know we're working together," he interrupted. "No one."

I grunted. "As if I'd ever want anyone to know. I have a reputation too, you know."

He huffed. "Right. Well, little wolf, I guess we'll be in touch. Stay out of trouble, please."

I smirked. "And what would be the fun in that?"

12

Instead of going home, I went to the Compound where I knew I'd find Bash—and most likely a pissed off Alexander and Ranulf since I ditched him this morning.

The door to the Compound was open and I walked right in. The first thing I noticed right off the bat was that there wasn't a Luna in sight. It was packed with male wolves, and the amount of kinetic energy in the room was palpable. Something was going on.

I found Jackson in the middle of the throng by the flat screen TV and squeezed my way through the crowd to get to him.

I tugged on his shirt when I reached him. "Jack, what's going on?"

"Kenz!" he said, his eyes widening in surprise. "You shouldn't be here. All Lunas are in their rooms. Let me take you to mine, where Amy is—"

He started to tug me forward, but I dug in my heels. "Why?"

His chocolate eyes turned irritated. "Because it's about to get really violent in a couple minutes, and the Lycans in here may lose control."

I scanned the crowd of Lycans and saw what Jackson was talking about. The wall of testosterone was fused with building energy, and the looks on their faces said they were ready for a fight. I'd only been gone a couple hours that morning; I couldn't have missed *that* much. What happened?

I found Ollie standing on the other side of the living room by the French doors that led to the back yard. "Ollie!" I yelled over the crowd. I tore myself from Jackson's grasp and went to my brother, pushing past everyone in my way.

"Kenzie, what are you doing here?" he said as he took hold of me. "They took all the women away. You can't be here—"

I smiled. He still wasn't used to calling them Lunas. He was still so human. "I just got here. Have you seen Bash? Alexander?"

"I think they're in his office." He put an arm around me as some wolves started pushing and bumping into others in the surrounding area.

I looked outside through the glass of the French doors and saw Sterling in the backyard with Mohammad beside her, as if coaching her. I darted around Ollie and reached for the door handle and pushed it open, stepping outside.

"Sterling!" I yelled, catching her attention as I walked toward her and Mohammad.

"Kenz!" she beamed and met me halfway. "I'm so glad you're here!"

"What's happening?" I quirked a brow as my gaze traveled from her to Mohammad and back.

"Didn't Sebastian tell you?" She frowned. "I'm fighting for the position of Captain today."

Well, that explained a lot. No wonder the Pack was amped up with so much adrenaline. They were about to witness a blood-bath. But why weren't Lunas allowed to watch? A damn Luna was fighting! They should be able to witness history in the making.

"Why aren't the Lunas allowed to watch?" I asked, a little angrier than expected. I wasn't upset with Sterling. I shouldn't take it out on her.

"They are." Mohammad was the one to respond. He pointed up at the Compound behind me.

I turned around and looked at the second and third floors of the Compound, seeing Lunas with their faces plastered against the glass in all the windows that covered the back of the building, watching the backyard.

"The Lunas cannot be down here because the wolves are unpredictable, and we cannot protect them all if the wolves lose control. They are safer upstairs," Mohammad explained in his monotone voice. I looked into his dead eyes and a chill scampered down my spine. "You should make yourself scarce, Mackenzie. I can protect Sterling."

"No!" Sterling exclaimed. "I want her here!"

I smiled at her. "I'll be right here. I'm not going anywhere." I turned to the scary Captain. "I can handle myself just fine. Thank you, though."

"Great!" Sterling clapped her hands. "I'll be fighting Marshall first. He's very big and—"

"What have I told you about big men?" Mohammad cut her off.

"They're the weakest," she sighed. "I know, I know. But he's still intimidating," she muttered.

I watched them interact and wondered if I made the right

choice by agreeing to have Mohammad train Sterling. Not that it was my choice, but maybe I could have fought a little harder for her. I guessed I would find out during this first fight how well he'd prepared her.

Sterling was an excellent fighter when she trained with me. She was five feet, eleven inches tall and extremely muscular for a woman, which intimidated all the male wolves in the Pack, but made me love her even more. I wouldn't lie, I had a little girl crush on Sterling Rose. She was badass. And with Mohammad as her mentor, she could be unstoppable.

"How nice of you to join us," Bash said from behind me. I turned around to face him as he walked out of the Compound to the backyard where we stood. He was followed by Jackson and Ollie.

"You could have told me, you know."

"I would have, if you hadn't disappeared this morning," he said with a knowing look that told me we'd be discussing this later when we didn't have an audience. "Your father and Ranulf are back at home waiting for you, and I told them you'd be there once this is over."

"Thank you." I smiled and leaned up to Bash, giving him a peck on the cheek.

"Are you sure you want her around, boss? She can watch with Amy from my room," Jackson suggested, to which I responded with the stink eye.

Bash shook his head. "She'll be fine. I'll be by her side, and Mackenzie isn't exactly helpless. You should know that by now."

I could kiss him right now. I gave Bash a beaming smile that promised oh so many things tonight. I loved when he let me handle myself because I knew it took a lot for him to do it. He had to override every wolf instinct he had.

"Let's get this started," Bash said. "Allow the wolves outside and bring me Marshall."

Jackson nodded and jogged to the French doors, whistling to get everyone's attention. The wolves came outside in droves to the grassy backyard, forming a circle around us. There were roughly fifty wolves present.

Cutting through the crowd, Jackson appeared with who I assumed was Marshall. Sterling was right, he was a very big man. Standing at the same height as Ollie, he was completely beefed up, like he was on steroids or something. His shirtless torso showcased veins popping out of his muscled arms. He flexed them and growled as he neared Sterling, giving her a feral look. He had stringy black hair that was held back by a tie, but some strands had come loose. Everything about him screamed *rabid animal*. He would be one heck of a fighter. I couldn't believe *this* guy wanted to be a captain.

As Sebastian spoke with Marshall, I took the opportunity to have a little pep talk with Sterling.

"You got this, Sterling." I grabbed her by the shoulders and turned her to face me. "Strength is not in the size of the arms, but in the size of the brain. Remember that. You can outsmart him. He will fight you with brute strength, and that's why he'll lose. You're stealthier than that. You understand?"

She nodded and gulped. I saw the fear etched on her face.

"Fear is in the mind." I pointed to the side of her head. "We control our minds, which means you control your fears. I've never had as much faith in someone as I do you, Sterling Rose."

"What if I can't do it?" she mumbled.

"With that attitude, you won't be able to. You can and *will* become Captain. Say it with me."

She looked into my eyes. "I will become Captain."

"Good. Now say it like you mean it."

"I will become Captain!" she vowed.

I grinned. "Damn right you will. Now go kick that juice monkey's ass!"

She growled and her canines slipped out. Sterling turned to the inner circle where Marshall and Sebastian were waiting for her. She stepped forward, cracking her neck and knuckles.

"This is not a fight to the death," Bash said. "No killing blows. If that happens, you're disqualified and there will be consequences. If you can't handle it anymore, you tap out. Do I make myself clear?"

Marshall grunted and Sterling nodded.

I stepped back and blended with the crowd to give them space. The others did the same until it was only Sterling and Marshall in the middle of the circle. Bash came to stand beside me.

"Begin!" he shouted, his voice booming across the back yard like a canon.

The surrounding Lycans started yelling and throwing their fists in the air, cheering Marshall on, who went on the offensive immediately. He charged for Sterling, his tree trunk arms spread out wide with his claws out, but she ducked and easily swerved out of his way, dipping under his arms and around him. She glided like a ninja as she missed every attack aimed her way. But she wouldn't win if she stayed on the defensive.

"Come on, Sterling!" I shouted, earning a few growls from the

Lycans around me. "Go on the offense!" I crouched, putting my hands on my knees as I watched the fight intently.

Sterling slid between his legs, popping up behind him and jabbing her elbow into his spine, then she stomped her foot on the back of his knee, making him jerk as if he were about to fall to a knee, but she didn't hit him hard enough.

"Climb on his back!" I yelled, pointing to his back as if she could see me. "Headlock!"

She reacted too slow and he turned and back handed her, knocking her into the unsympathetic crowd, which tossed her back into the circle. Blood dripped from her nose and lip.

Sterling was a better fighter than this—at least she was when she fought Lunas. I'd never compared her against a male wolf who had been fighting all his life, unlike the Lunas. Hadn't she fought against Mohammad to prepare for this? I peered over at the Captain who stood stoically, his back ramrod straight and his expression neutral as he watched the fight. He gave nothing away. He must have sensed me looking at him because he turned in my direction and narrowed his eyes, then turned back to the fight.

Sterling was getting hit hard. Her face was already bruised and bloody, and her steps were slow. This wasn't good. If she didn't gain the upper hand quickly, she'd be tapping out soon.

Marshall grabbed her by the neck and lifted her off the ground, leaving only her tiptoes grazing the grass. He was choking her, not enough to kill her, but enough for her to tap out.

She gripped his wrist and her face turned red as she stared at me with wide eyes over his shoulder. Any moment now, she would tap out and it would be over. The wolves around us howled and cheered gleefully. I peered up at the windows of the

Compound and saw the distraught faces of the Lunas. They needed this win. So did Sterling.

What could she do that wouldn't be considered a killing move? *Fuck.* I racked my brain and just as I saw her raise her hand, I screamed.

"My signature move!" I shouted over the noise. I couldn't step into the circle while the fight was in motion, and Bash's hand was gripping my arm to hold me back because I was itching to go in. "Do my signature move! You know the one!"

Her brows furrowed and I nodded at her, giving her a smirk. I saw the moment the light bulb went off in her head and we finally connected. She knew what I meant.

"What are you ranting about?" Bash whispered in my ear. I ignored him, never taking my eyes off Sterling.

Her hands went to Marshall's shoulders and she rammed her knee in his groin — hard. The wolf released her immediately, dropping to the ground as he cupped his crotch.

"Now, Sterling!" I yelled.

She gasped, sucking in a lungful of air before stalking toward him and punching him in the throat, then wrapping her thick arm around his neck. Sterling dropped to the ground and tightened her hold, squeezing as he fought, but he was hurt and wasn't as strong as he once was. They tussled on the ground for a bit, but she wasn't letting go. When he realized that, his hand tapped her arm and Bash stepped into the circle and raised his hand, ending the fight.

"Sterling Rose is our victor for round one!" he shouted. Sterling released Marshall as Bash's voice rang out in the air.

She fell onto her back, gulping air, and I darted to her side. The assembled Lycans didn't like that verdict. The growls and snarls were getting louder by the second, and the pushes became shoves as the crowd boiled. It was starting to look like a damn mosh pit.

"Sterling!" I dropped to my knees beside her. "Are you okay?"

Her chest rose rapidly. "I just need to … catch my breath."

I chuckled. "Take all the time you need. You deserve it."

"Thank you." She turned her head in my direction. "I couldn't have done it without you."

"I didn't do a thing. It was all you, Sterling. You kicked ass, just like I thought you would."

Sterling sat up slowly and I helped her to her feet. The circle was getting smaller by the second as the wolves got rowdier.

"We better get her out of here," Mohammad said as he came to her other side. "She needs to get cleaned up for her next fight, and the wolves need time to calm down."

I nodded and watched Mohammad carefully lift her into his arms and carry her out of the backyard. He snarled at anyone who got in his way and the wolves parted like the Red Sea for him. I guessed I wasn't the only one who was nervous around him.

"It'll only get harder from here," Jackson voiced as he came to stand beside me. "She got lucky with Marshall."

I ran a hand through my hair. "She'll get through this. How many more wolves does she have to fight?"

"Two more," he said. "And they'll be tougher on her because she's a Luna. They want to prove Lunas don't belong in positions of authority."

"Lovely," I deadpanned. "Sterling is going to be fine."

"And if she's not?"

I gave him an annoyed look. "It's *my* job to be pessimistic. Stop." I slapped him on the chest.

He shrugged. "I'm just preparing you for reality. I know she has something to prove and she's tough as nails, but these wolves are no joke, either. They're on another level."

"Could I fight them?" I peered up at Jackson. "Would I stand a chance against these so-called, other level wolves?"

He rolled his eyes. "You're different, Kenz—"

"No I'm not! This is the problem. You don't see Lunas as equals—not even to me. Sterling is just like me, probably even stronger. But none of you will give her a chance because of what's between her legs."

"That's not fair, Kenz. I never said—"

"You didn't have to, Jackson," I sighed. "I know you're one of the more progressive of the bunch and you don't mean to, but you're wired to think Lunas are weak, no matter what. Which is why you won't even contemplate the possibility that Sterling might actually win this and become your colleague. Just have some hope, Jack. Please." I reached for his hand and he squeezed it.

He grinned. "You're such a pain in my ass, Kenz."

"But this pain in the ass is right, ain't she?" I raised a brow.

He groaned. "Yes, you're probably right with your psycho-analysis. Fine. Sterling might have a chance. But she needs to think about her next move faster. She's lagging during the fight, which is how Marshall got the upper hand so quickly."

I nodded. "I agree. I'll talk to her."

I squeezed his hand once more and let him go. I turned to the rowdy crowd of wolves and dove in, pushing my way through them. I was pushed, elbowed, and even dodged a fist. I didn't understand why they were so amped up, but it would only get worse with two more fights to go.

"Move!" I yelled as I jabbed my elbow into someone. The wolf tried to backhand me, but I grabbed his wrist before it connected and twisted it in an unnatural way. "Not nice," I growled.

"Bitch!" he snarled.

I twisted even more. "Well, that's just plain mean." I kicked him in the gut and he flew into a crowd of wolves that began tossing him around. I cut through the remaining group, evading more fists and the occasional hair pull, and finally made it to the French doors that led inside the Compound.

I passed through the empty living room and hurried upstairs where I found all the Lunas gathered in the hallway talking excitedly.

"Oh my gosh, did you see her?"

"She was amazing!"

"Sterling's totally going to win!"

"Will they allow it? The King is here, you know."

"They have to follow the rules!"

Multiple conversations filtered down the corridor as I tried to find the room Sterling was in. Their excitement was palpable—they had faith in her to win. Even with the minor setback she had, they still had hope. It was the greatest feeling ever, and Sterling needed to know what the Lunas were feeling. It would help her in the upcoming fights.

I peered through multiple doors, scanned empty bedrooms, and was moving on to the third floor where I ran into more Lunas. Amy was at the end of the hallway and I hurried to her side. She was dressed for summertime in cut-off shorts and a tank, her flaming red curls piled into a messy bun, her myriad of tattoos on full display. Her pierced face brightened when she saw me.

"Kenzie! I thought I saw you down there," she said as I approached.

"Yeah, I came by pure coincidence. I didn't know today was the fight, but I'm glad I'm here. Have you seen Sterling?"

Amy nodded. "I let her and Mohammad use Jackson's room to clean up until the next fight."

"Perfect." I gave Amy a kiss on the top of her head. "You're a saint."

She shrugged. "How about you owe me a trip to Gray's Papaya, and we call it even?"

I grinned. "Deal."

I backtracked to the second floor, leaving Amy behind as I headed to Jackson's room. The door was locked, so I knocked and waited for someone to open it.

"It's Mackenzie," I said through the door. "Open up!"

The lock clicked and the door swung open. I hurried in and shut the door, locking it. Sterling was in wolf form, pacing the room like a caged animal.

I didn't think Amy really thought this through when she offered up Jackson's room. I looked around and took in his massive bed with silk sheets, his gaming area with every console you could think of with multiple games lying around, and a gamer chair in front of a huge flat screen TV. Jackson would lose his shit if anything was destroyed.

"Is she okay?" I asked Mohammad, who stood behind me quietly.

"She's healing, but she's agitated."

"She needs to be quicker. Her reaction time is too slow." I watched her pace the room.

"I am aware," he said pensively.

"What are we going to do?"

"*We?*" He came around to stand in front of me and raised a brow. "You helped her in her last fight, but it was a cheap shot—"

"It's survival," I growled. "Don't minimize her victory because it was a hit to the dick."

Nothing I said fazed him.

"Nonetheless, her next opponent will be expecting that move. It only works once."

He wasn't wrong. Her other two competitors would have watched her first fight and observed her fighting style, if they were smart. They had the upper hand. She had to step up her game. A knee to the groin wouldn't work again. Not in this fight, at least.

"I'll do better," Sterling said, and we both turned to look at her naked form by Jackson's bed. She'd just shifted back and was putting her clothes back on. "I wasn't ready for the first fight, but I'm ready now. I know what to expect."

I stepped around Mohammad and went to her. "In real life, there are no practice fights. It's life or death, Sterling. You should have given it all you had."

Her brows furrowed. "I did—I *thought* I did."

"The Lunas are counting on you, Sterling. You should hear them," I muttered. "You're a hero to them. Don't let them down."

She chuckled. "No pressure."

I smirked. "Welcome to my world."

After some breathing exercises and a pep talk from Mohammad that I wasn't privy to, we made our way back downstairs. Once we exited the room, the Lunas erupted in cheers. Sterling blushed crimson from the attention. It was endearing to see. The Lunas needed a champion; someone besides me.

When we arrived downstairs, the wolves had simmered down and we were able to cut through the crowd and get to the inner circle easily with Mohammad as our guide. Bash was waiting for us with the next opponent. He was smaller than Marshall, but still bigger than Sterling—although not by much.

"Who is he?" I asked Sterling when we stopped in the middle.

"Trayvon," she said. "He's fairly new to the Pack. Only been in for a year or so, but he was a Captain in his last Pack, so he has an advantage. He's actually really nice."

I could see in her distressed face that she liked him, maybe a little more than friends. I followed her gaze to Trayvon, who smiled and nodded at Bash as he listened to the instructions. He could be the nicest guy on earth, but right now he was the enemy and she needed to be ready to defeat him.

"Look at me, Sterling." I gripped her arm. "I don't care if he owns a damn orphanage and feeds the homeless every weekend, he is the enemy."

Her face tightened. "Yes."

"Kick his ass with no remorse. Don't hold back."

She shook her head. "I won't."

"Good. Now go take another step at becoming Captain."

She nodded and went to meet Bash and Trayvon in the middle of the circle. I blended in with the crowd alongside Mohammad and waited for the fight to begin. When it did, Trayvon didn't strike immediately. He waited patiently for Sterling to make the first move. She lunged for him, but he employed a stealthier approach. When he swerved out of the way of her lunge, he punched her in the side. I winced as I watched her curve into herself and gasp for air.

Bash held me and brought his mouth to my ears. "You can't help her this time. I had to calm a lot of wolves after you left because of your assistance. Keep quiet."

My head snapped in his direction. He gave me a stern look that I returned with a glare, but I knew he was right. I had to let her do this alone. She wouldn't always have me with her out on the field, if ever. As Captain, she'd have to hold her own.

I nodded stiffly and returned my attention to the fight. My fists were clenched at my side and I knew crescent moons were indented in my palms from my nails.

Sterling got in two punches to his face and swept his leg, knocking him down. *She got the advantage!* I inched forward and had to stop myself from moving any further.

She straddled Trayvon and started wailing on him. He attempted to cover his face, but she was too fast. *Good ... keep going.* He lifted his hips up and bucked her off him, but she wrapped her legs around his waist in a fluid wrestling move. Without pausing, she locked his arms and bent them into an unnatural position as they laid on the ground. I was expecting him to yell uncle by the way she had him pinned.

She pulled against his arms tighter and he screamed in pain, his free hand tapping the ground frantically to end the fight. *Damn, she did it.* Sterling released him and when they stood, he did something that surprised me completely—he shook her hand in appreciation. Maybe there was hope for the male Lycan population, after all.

Sterling bounced up and ran toward us and I pulled her into a hug. "You did it!"

"I think I broke a couple ribs, though," she wheezed as she lifted her shirt to show me a bruise starting to bloom on her side.

"Shift before your next fight. Who's your next opponent?" I looked around at the crowd, searching the faces for one who stood out.

She looked nervous. "He didn't tell you?"

"Who tell me what?"

Sterling looked behind her and then back at me. "I have to fight Sebastian."

13

"Say what?" I exclaimed, stumbling back in surprise.

Sterling bit her lip nervously. "The last fight is with the Alpha. You're not expected to win, but it's mainly how long you can last."

That sounded completely barbaric. He was going to beat her to a bloody pulp just to see how long she could withstand it? That was some gang-type shit. She couldn't do that! She made it this far, wasn't that enough?

"That's ridiculous, Sterling." I shook my head. "You can't do that. I'll talk to Bash—"

"No!" she shouted. "I have to. Marshall and Trayvon will fight next, and then the winner of the two will fight Bash as well. Whichever one of us lasts longer will get the position of Captain. I have to do it, Kenz!"

The whole thing sounded completely absurd. Who the hell made up these rules? We lived in the twenty-first century, for God's sake! They needed to update them ASAP.

Mohammad pulled Sterling away and they walked back into the Compound while I stood there dumbfounded, wondering what the hell was going on around me. When I spoke to Bash about her fight, he never mentioned this part. He should have, but he knew I wouldn't agree. He was choosing his battles with me much more carefully.

Just as the fight between Marshall and Trayvon was about to begin, I sent Bash a glare and left the backyard through the side gate instead of going through the house. From his glowing eyes, I knew he was aware that I knew.

I stepped over weeds and patches of dirt as I passed the side of the Compound and headed to the gate, unhooking the latch and opening it to exit the yard. I walked to our house where I knew Alexander and Ranulf were waiting for me. I couldn't solve Sterling's problem right now, so I'd handle mine.

Keys in hand, I jogged up the steps to the front door and inserted the keys in the lock and twisted the knob. I opened the door, closed it behind me, and locked it again. I heard their footsteps immediately and met them at the entrance of the foyer and living room.

"Mackenzie!" Alexander exclaimed, his gray eyes turning silver. "Where have ye been?"

I scratched my head. "I just came from the Brooklyn Pack's Compound. They're having the fights for the Captain position, and my friend is participating—"

"Before that," Ranulf interrupted. His eyes were hard. I could tell he was not happy with me.

I sighed. "I got a lead on the case I'm working on. I had to do it alone, no offense."

"Offense taken," Ranulf barked. "Don ye leave like that again, ye hear, ye stupid girl? Ye could have been dead, for all we knew. Ye had yer Da worried sick! Have ye no consideration—"

Alexander held up a hand. "Enough, Ranulf."

I pinched the bridge of my nose and closed my eyes, holding off a migraine that was marching toward my temples. "I swear I'm not trying to be difficult, but you can't just waltz to New York and expect me to bend at your will! You know I won't do that."

"Yer right, darling, I cannae come to yer home and expect ye to do as I say, but I expect ye to want to stay alive. Which means being careful, and yer nae," Alexander chastised, urging me to follow him into the living room.

I followed him, passing an angry Ranulf. "I was perfectly safe this morning," I lied. He didn't need to know about having to be rescued by Úlfur—again. No one needed to know about that.

"Ye should be bringing back-up with ye every time ye go out," Alexander added as he sat down on the sofa. I sat beside him. "There was no excuse as for why ye didn't bring Ranulf with ye. From now on, he goes where ye go, no exceptions. Nae until this threat is removed."

This was going to be a problem. Úlfur wouldn't show up with Ranulf around, and after this conversation, I couldn't willfully ditch the Lycan again.

"Ye will be Queen soon, Mackenzie." Alexander took my hand. "Ye have to be more careful. Yer life is worth more now than ever before. Yer the last MacCoinnich."

"Okay ... I'm sorry. I won't do it again," I relented. I would have to think of something soon, but for now, I'd keep him happy with a concession. "Can I talk to you about something else?"

His silver eyes faded to gray and softened, pleased that he'd gotten what he wanted. "Anything, darling."

"Who makes the rules for the fights for Pack positions?" I asked not very casually.

He tilted his head. "It is borne of traditions passed down through the generations. I don know exactly who created it. Why?"

I gnawed at my lower lip, wondering if I should tell him or not. "I have a friend fighting today—"

"That's wonderful!" Alexander beamed, patting my knee. "I hope he's doing well."

I shut my eyes. Of course, he thought it was a man. "No, Alexander, it's a Luna that's fighting." I reopened my eyes to look at his expression.

He jerked back in shock. "Crivvens, how did *that* happen?"

I rolled my eyes. "Your new laws allow it, remember?"

"Bloody hell, but I didnae think they'd want to be Captains! Sebastian should nae have allowed it."

"Alexander!" I yelled. "This is exactly what we fought for – the right to be anything – and if Sterling wants to be Captain, then she should be able to fight for it. But the old ways are barbaric!"

His head snapped in my direction. "The fighting bothers ye?"

"The part where they have to fight the Alpha bothers me. There's no way she'll win against Bash, and besides that, it's about how long she can last. How is that right?"

Alexander stood and adjusted his tie. "This has been done for centuries, Mackenzie. Are ye trying to ask for an exception for a Luna?" He raised a brow.

I was about to say something but stopped myself, my mouth hanging open. Ranulf chuckled in the corner of the room. I was asking for a special privilege, and for what? Because she was a Luna? The male wolves had endured this since the beginning of time. Even if it was barbaric, they survived. Sterling could, too. Funny how she knew that before I did. I was just too protective of her. Oh, how the tables had turned.

"You're right," I muttered. "I didn't think of it that way."

Alexander sighed. "I know ye want to protect them, lass, but ye have to let them get hurt sometimes. It's the only way they'll learn."

With that little nugget, I left the house completely defeated with Ranulf trailing behind me. Alexander was right; they had to hurt sometimes to know what it was like in the real world. It was why Sterling wasn't ready for her first fight. She had been too protected in her bubble.

When we returned to the backyard, Ranulf pushed everyone out of the way by order of a royal decree, which really tamed the wolves, creating a clear path for me to walk through to the center where Bash was just finishing a fight with Trayvon. I guess he'd already won against Marshall.

I found Sterling standing with Mohammad and made my way to her side. I looked up at the building windows and saw all the Lunas peering down at us, smiling brightly, some with their camera phones at the ready.

A loud thud jerked me away from them to the circle where Trayvon's body dropped to the ground in a lump, unmoving. Jackson walked into the inner circle and raised his hand.

"Thirteen minutes and twenty-two seconds!" Jackson called out the time of the fight and the wolves howled and cheered. Bash wiped the blood from his knuckles on his jeans and mopped the sweat on his forehead with his forearm.

"I just have to make it past that," Sterling mumbled as she bounced on the balls of her feet anxiously.

"You can do this," I whispered, wishing I could help her but knowing I couldn't. Giving away any of Bash's weaknesses would be a betrayal to him and I wouldn't do it, not even for the Lunas.

"Thanks, Kenz." She peered down at me and then stepped into the circle as two wolves dragged Trayvon out.

I almost didn't want to watch. Bash made eye contact with me for a quick moment and then it was gone as he focused completely on Sterling. How he had enough stamina and strength without shifting between fights proved why he deserved to be Alpha.

Once the fight began, I couldn't wipe the grimace from my face as I watched them move. Sebastian was a beast and he didn't hold back because she was a Luna. He treated her like one of the guys. I appreciated it, but also felt really bad for Sterling. It was an odd feeling. She took every hit and kept her feet firmly on the ground. She even got a few punches in, to my surprise, and I couldn't tell if it was pure luck or if Bash allowed it. Sterling tried ducking out of the way, but he caught her around the waist, lifted her off the ground, and slammed her down. Her head bounced like a basketball and I winced. She should have tucked her chin to her chest, but she probably didn't see him coming fast enough. She gasped for the air that fled her lungs and scrambled away from him until she backed into some wolves who kicked her into the circle again.

I lost track of the time, but this fight felt like an eternity and I didn't know how much more I could take of it.

Sterling was wobbling on her feet as she stood before Bash, her weak arms barely able to protect her face. She was breathing heavily as Bash circled her like prey. He punched her twice in the stomach—right then left. She curved in on herself but stood upright, wheezing. Her hand clamped onto his shoulder to hold herself up and Bash swept her leg back, making her fall to the ground. With one swift punch to the face, she was knocked out cold.

Jackson stepped into the circle and raised his hand to simmer the out-of-control wolves, who were howling and clamoring for the verdict. As their voices lowered to hear the final results, I looked up at the windows to see the Lunas opening the windows, their phones out, recording the moment.

"Thirteen minutes," Jackson began, and I held my breath.

So far, the tally was the same as Trayvon, which meant it would all come down to seconds. I grabbed onto a random wrist for support and stood with bated breath, waiting for him to finish.

"... and twenty-nine seconds!" Jackson grinned and the crowd erupted.

I squealed like a schoolgirl as I squeezed the wrist I was holding and started to jump up and down. *She did it! She won!* If only she were awake to bask in the evidence of her greatness.

"Mackenzie," Mohammad said dryly, and I looked over at him. His gaze dropped to my hand, which was holding onto his wrist.

"Oh! Sorry," I grumbled and released him quickly. "She did it, Mohammad!"

"Yes, she did." He nodded, still expressionless.

The Lunas were yelling and cheering from the windows as the male wolves fought between each other, clearly upset with the verdict.

Mohammad strode over to Sterling's unconscious body,

picked her up, and carried her inside the Compound. I decided not to crowd them and just let him take care of her. He'd obviously been doing a good job thus far.

"This is only the beginning," Ranulf mumbled as he stood beside me, keeping guard. "They'll want more after this."

"As is their right," I said, turning to stare at him defiantly. "They deserve this."

He eyed me, calculating his next words. "Maybe yer right."

Jackson and the rest of the Captains calmed the crowd and made them disperse from the backyard. In just a few minutes, there were only a couple of us left. I was glad to see Ollie was one of them.

"There you are!" I gave him a one-armed hug. "How are you feeling?"

"I have a lot of adrenaline running through my veins," he admitted, seemingly confused by the experience.

"It's all the fighting," Bash clarified as he approached, taking off his shirt and wiping his sweat and blood with it. "Your wolf wants in on the action."

Ollie shook his head. "I don't like this feeling."

I gave him a sad smile. "It'll go away, I promise. Why don't we shift? A good run will get rid of that adrenaline." I turned to Bash and gave him a smirk. "She did good, didn't she?"

He grunted. "She did all right."

"Pfft. She did more than all right. She did better than Trayvon—"

"But Trayvon wouldn't have needed training to step up as Captain," Bash said. "She will. Sterling's lucky Mohammad took a liking to her and is willing to put in the extra effort."

I rolled my eyes. "Why can't you just appreciate the win? You're so bitter."

He sighed. "This won't be easy for her, Mackenzie. The other Captains won't make it easy for her. She has to be ready."

This wasn't over, that much was clear. She may have won the battle, but the war was far from over.

14

Getting away from the Compound was a smart move. The wolves were on a testosterone rampage after Sterling's win, and it took Sebastian's Alpha voice to calm them down. The Lunas were celebrating in private to not stir up any trouble, but they were waiting for Sterling to wake up to really celebrate. That girl was knocked out and had no idea she won. It was sort of funny.

In the meantime, I took Ollie to the park to shift. He was still too new and didn't understand all the emotions coursing through his body. He couldn't differentiate between his human and wolf feelings. Ranulf was with us (obviously), because I needed a babysitter—insert eye roll here. We were trying to find a spot to shift in Prospect Park, which was unusually empty of humans. We walked further into the woods and found the clearing where Bash and I typically shifted.

"This is a good spot," I said and started to lift my shirt.

"Whoa! Kenz!" Ollie turned away from me quickly and covered his eyes.

I started to laugh. *Right, this would be awkward for him.* I was so used to it by now that I'd forgotten he'd probably feel uncomfortable.

"Sorry." I pulled my shirt down again. "How about we shift in different areas? Are you capable of shifting on your own?"

He peeked over his shoulder, and then fully turned around when he saw I was still dressed. "I don't know," he admitted as he ran a hand through his hair.

"I'll go with him," Ranulf offered. "We won't be far, and I'll still be able to hear ye if anything is near."

"Thank you," I replied with relief. I didn't want to send Ollie to shift by himself, but I knew he'd be uncomfortable seeing me naked, even though I saw him during his first shift. Those were different circumstances, though.

They walked deeper into the woods, and with my acute hearing I heard them settle just beyond a couple nearby bushes. Ranulf wasn't lying, he really didn't intend to stray far from me. He wasn't taking any chances that I'd sneak off.

I pulled my shirt over my head and neatly folded it, placing it on the ground. I was starting to take off my bra when I heard a rustle behind me. My head snapped in that direction and I waited for whatever was coming toward me to show itself. If it was a human, it was going to get real awkward, real quick.

The bushes rustled and then spread apart and someone stepped through. I saw a mop of dark hair, and when he lifted his head, I relaxed.

"Úlfur," I sighed. "What are *you* doing here?" I whispered, knowing Ranulf was listening. I tapped my ear and pointed in the guard's direction to let Úlfur know we weren't alone.

"Twice in one day, little wolf. This must be a record," he whispered back with a grin. I'd just seen him this morning. "I was following the Skofnung stone. It's here."

My eyes widened. "I thought it was in the fae realm?"

"It *was* in the fae realm. Now it's here. It's on the move, and your human is close to retrieving it."

That wasn't possible. How the hell could a human be so damn powerful and capable of acquiring all those relics? If I didn't stop him and fast, no one would be able to.

"How was Cardona able to get the stone?"

"It was sold on the black market. Once all the objects started being stolen, I guess the owner thought better of it and decided to sell instead of getting killed for it." Úlfur scanned the clearing. "The trade is happening now. We have to act fast, little wolf."

I couldn't ditch Ranulf—not so soon, at least. I also needed to alert the SIU. This was our best chance of capturing Billie Cardona. If we caught him in the act of illegally purchasing the Skofnung stone, we'd have a case against him. Other than that, we had nothing. We couldn't search his place without a warrant, and we wouldn't be able to get one without showing probable cause. And let's be real – no judge in the city would sign that warrant, not against the Commissioner.

"Where is the deal going down?" I looked back in the direction Ranulf and Ollie had gone.

"The rose garden."

I quirked a brow. The rose garden was a part of Prospect Park that had fallen into disarray and hadn't grown a rose in years. It was under renovation. What was it with the Commissioner and places of restoration?

"I have a bodyguard here with me; I can't ditch him. He's with my brother," I said, biting my lower lip.

Úlfur tilted his head. "You have a brother? Interesting."

I stiffened. I shouldn't have told him that. Why did I open my damn mouth? "Stay the hell away from him," I growled.

Úlfur smirked and lifted his hands placatingly. "I mean you no harm, little wolf. Let me handle your people. Go ahead to the rose garden; I'll meet you there."

I frowned. "I don't trust you not to hurt them."

"I won't," he said. "I promise."

"Your promise means nothing to me." I looked behind me once more and then at Úlfur. "If you hurt them, I'll kill you." Even I knew that was an empty threat.

He gave me his trademark mischievous smirk. "I wouldn't have it any other way."

Without overthinking it further, I hurried out of the clearing and toward the rose garden. It was on the northeast corner of the park, which meant I'd have to hurry. I snatched up my shirt and put it on as I ran.

The rest of the park was eerily devoid of humans, and I wondered if it had anything to do with the trade that was about to happen. I pumped my arms harder as I hustled to get to the other side of the park in record time. I didn't know how Úlfur intended to *handle* my people, but he was something *else*.

Sweat rolled down my spine. The heat was unbearable, even though the sun was setting. When I approached the perimeter of the rose garden, I stayed within the bushes, not wanting to make myself known until I had to. I visualized the layout of the rose garden: a sunken, concrete circle in the center that dipped two feet, surrounded by rose bushes. I strained my wolf hearing for voices or the entrance of Úlfur, but couldn't hear anything yet.

I squatted on the ground and made a hole in the branches to see what was going on, but there was no one there. I pulled out my phone and sent a quick text to Cassidy.

The stone is being traded. The rose garden—Prospect Park. Stay hidden.

I hit send and switched my phone to silent so no one with sensitive hearing would hear it ring or vibrate. Slipping it in my back pocket, I surveyed the area for anything unusual, however the only thing unusual was how quiet it was. Then again, the rose garden was situated in a more secluded part of the park. It used to be filled with roses, but now there wasn't a single one. It had been pretty much abandoned, and now the city was trying to restore it to its former glory.

Suddenly, the wind picked up and leaves started to blow everywhere. In the center of the concrete circle, a shimmering, golden yellow swirl appeared. What began as a circle the size of a quarter grew until it was large enough to accommodate several people.

It was a portal. *Holy shit!*

Three fae emerged from the portal. Instead of closing behind them, the portal stayed open. I knew automatically what kind of creatures they were by their pointy ears, but fae also maintained an otherworldly look that always gave them away, almost as if they wore a filter. It was weird. The fae in the middle was holding a brown wooden box with golden latches.

They stood around for a minute before the Commissioner sauntered through the entrance to the rose garden and stepped down into the concrete circle. Not surprisingly, he didn't arrive alone; he was flanked by four others. I didn't know what they were, but they surrounded the circle without entering, standing sentinel at the edges.

"Did you bring it?" Cardona asked greedily.

"Of course," the fae in the center responded. He had long, silky white hair that flowed to the middle of his back. "Did you bring what we asked for?"

"Of course," Cardona mimicked. With a snap of his fingers, hands suddenly gripped my arms and lifted me off the ground.

"Hey!" I whisper-yelled, but it was no use. My captors pushed their way through the bushes and brought me out into the rose garden.

"Ah, here she is, as you requested," Cardona said to the fae. The Commissioner looked at me. "Did you really think we were meeting here by coincidence? I've had a tracking spell placed on you for days."

I cursed, belatedly realizing it would certainly have been strange for the trade to take place where I was shifting. The world was a small place, but it wasn't *that* small. Nothing was ever that convenient.

Now the big question was, what the hell did the fae want with me? Did they really hate me that much for killing Drusilla?

"Don't give him that stone!" I yelled at the fae. "I'll come to you willingly if you refuse him!"

Cardona snorted. "I have you. If they want you, they'll give me what I want. There are no side negotiations here, Mackenzie."

I flailed against the two guys who held me, but they were strong as hell. Were they Lycan?

The trade was about to take place, and I couldn't let that

happen. Without thinking it through, I went into a half shift, emitting a loud growl that vibrated through my chest. I did a back flip and twisted their arms, forcing them to release me. Once they did, I dug my claws deep into their abdomens. They caved into themselves and gasped as I pulled out their entrails.

I raced for the box, jumping down into the circle and snatching it out of the fae's hand before it could be transferred to Cardona.

"Bitch!" the Commissioner shouted. "Give that to me now!"

I gripped it tightly to my side with bloody hands. "You're not getting *dick!*" I scanned the surrounding area and watched as his bodyguards moved to surround me, the fae watching with a detached air. I didn't have an exit strategy. I could try to go through their portal, but who knew where it would take me? I couldn't take that risk.

"Get her! And get me my stone," Cardona snarled, spurring his guards into action.

I didn't have a way out, and with the box firmly in my grasp, I was now fighting with one hand. I refused to let it go.

The first one who approached me was a warlock. I ducked and swerved to avoid his magic ... and stepped right into the next one who wrapped his arms around me. Head-butting him with the back of my head, he loosened his hold on me and I stomped my foot on his and kicked his shin with all my might. He released me immediately. Not willing to take the risk of him regrouping, I swiped my claw across his throat and ripped it out. Before he fell, I held him up and used him as a shield as more magic was lobbed my way.

His body was heavy, and with only one arm to support him, I could only hold him up for so long. I edged around the circle with him until I couldn't anymore and dropped him, just missing another magic ball that arced over my head.

I was about to hop out of the circle when a growling wolf flew over my head and attacked the warlock, going straight for the jugular. It was a wolf I recognized. A dark brown coat with highlights and glowing yellow eyes—Ollie. He was savage as he tore into the warlock.

Ranulf bolted into the garden in a half-shift and attacked the last guard left standing. I didn't know where the fourth one was, which concerned me.

"You're outnumbered, Cardona," I yelled as I held on to the box. "Turn yourself in."

He laughed. "Outnumbered? Turn myself in? Dear, my people are scattered throughout this park. *You're* the one who's outmatched."

The Commissioner stepped toward the portal and looked over his shoulder at me. "I'll be coming for the stone." Then he disappeared into the portal.

Two of the fae followed, leaving the white-haired one. He turned to me, his eyes a beautiful lavender color. "Mackenzie MacCoinnich."

"What do you want?" I said unkindly.

"We mean you no harm."

"That's not what it looked like. You bargained for my life!"

He shook his head slightly. "Only to keep you safe. There is a bounty on your head, but we want you alive. You are set to be Queen, no?"

I frowned. This was confusing. "Yes?" I said it more like a question than a statement.

"The fae have helped Lycan royalty in the past. We wish to bestow upon you great power—"

"No," Ranulf interrupted. "A deal with the fae is a deal with the devil."

I'd already been bestowed with *great power* from the fae because of the magic they'd blessed our bloodline with. I was born a hybrid – a Lycan and an Oracle. Not many people knew my secret, and we kept it that way for reasons of safety, mainly for the Oracles. Whatever the fae were up to, it wasn't anything good. I certainly didn't need them to *bestow* anything else upon me. They'd given me enough.

"I appreciate the offer, but I politely decline," I said. "And I'm keeping the stone."

He bowed. "As you wish, Mackenzie MacCoinnich."

I didn't correct him. I just appreciated that he didn't call me Queen Slayer. I had so many nicknames, I needed a damn directory at this point. But I watched as he stepped through the portal and the portal closed behind him. The angry wind disappeared, as if a vacuum was shut off.

"Well, *that* was weird." I turned to Ranulf and Ollie.

"Mackenzie," Ranulf growled, "how many times have I told ye to stop running off?"

"In my defense, I knew you'd follow me, so was I really running off?" I shrugged and held up my hands, pleading my case.

Ranulf looked like he was going to blow a gasket. His face turned bright red and his nostrils flared, and I could practically see steam blowing out of those ears.

I kneeled in front of Ollie and scratched behind his ear. "You did amazing, big bro." I grinned. "Way to have my back."

He licked his canines in response and nodded. I hugged him and he nuzzled in my arms. I was taking a huge risk being this close with him, especially after a kill, but he was doing so good. He was a natural.

"Let's get him back to his clothes," Ranulf grunted.

I stood and we took a shadowy pathway back to the other side of the park to the clearing where we had started. I kept my ears open and clutched the box that contained the stone, waiting to hear any sign of Úlfur. But he was gone. He never showed.

15

After a much-needed shower to remove all the blood and grime from the park, Ranulf and I headed straight to the SIU with the Skofnung stone. Cas never made it to Prospect Park, so I messaged him and told him to meet me at the station.

We took side streets and stuck to the shadows in case we were being followed. When we made it to SIU's front desk, I waited impatiently while Ranulf showed them his passport so they could give him a visitor's pass, and then stepped into the elevator on our way to the squad room.

"Grey!" Michaels shouted as soon as he spotted me. It was apparent they were waiting on me, huddled as they were in the space between their desks.

"Hey!" I answered brightly as I approached, Ranulf stopping by the door to stand guard. "Thanks for coming on such short notice. It's been a crazy day."

"So we heard," Finn said. "You got the stone?"

"I stole it," I snorted. "Cardona was trying to buy it from the fae. Guess what their price was?"

Everyone shrugged and stared at me, waiting for the answer.

"Me."

"The fae wanted *you* in exchange for the stone?" Cas exclaimed.

I nodded. "They said they didn't want to hurt me, but I take everything they say with a grain of salt. Anyway, I snagged the stone and Cardona disappeared through a portal, but he said he'd be coming for it."

Michaels rubbed a hand across his mouth, pensive. "Can't we go after him for this? This should be enough for probable cause."

"He's the Commissioner," Briggs's voice bellowed in the somewhat empty squad room. We all turned to see him at the entryway of his office. "We're going to need much more to convict him."

"Can't we get Captain Voight involved?" I asked as a last-ditch effort. He was the Captain of the SIU and a well-respected warlock from Long Island. He was one of us.

Briggs gave me a sour look. "I've talked to Voight. He can't get involved—"

"Why not?" Finn yelled, aggravation clear in his voice.

"Because the rumors of corruption in the SIU are not just rumors!" Briggs shouted. He took deep, calming breaths and ran a hand over his bald head. "They have Voight by the proverbial balls. No point in asking Chief Brown, either."

My mouth hung slightly open and I couldn't believe what I was hearing, although I wasn't that surprised, either. We'd been hearing rumors for quite some time, and whenever we got calls to The Third Eye, everything just magically went away. We could never get to the puppet masters. Now we knew Maximos was a player, but who was controlling him? Was it the Commissioner? It just sounded completely absurd that a human could wield that much power over supernaturals.

"Then we don't ask them for shit," I said. "We have the stone and we know Cardona is coming for it, so we use it as bait to capture him. He said he's had a tracking spell on me for days, so we use it to our advantage. Let's think of a plan; a *good* one, because we'll only get one shot. Let's get this son of a bitch."

My three partners nodded their heads in agreement. Briggs, on the other hand, needed some convincing.

"It won't be that easy, Grey," he said in his gruff voice. "Cardona's not stupid. He won't fall for the bait that easily. Hell, he might not even be the one to come after you. He'll probably send someone else to do his dirty work."

"Which is why we'll also be looking for the other two objects he stole while he's busy searching for the stone. Deflection." I tapped a finger on the side of my head. "He won't expect us to come for him from the front and the back."

"It'll be difficult to search all the properties he owns," Finn said, "and he'll be able to track our progress by the warrants we pull to search."

"Not necessarily." Cas furrowed his brows. "Cardona is the gloating type. He'd want his spoils near him at all times. We just need to follow him. We can get some wolves he won't recognize to track him. That way, we won't need to search the system for him."

"What if you're wrong?" Michaels asked.

"We'll cross that bridge when we get there." Cas shrugged. "But I'm almost positive I'm right."

I nodded. It was true – Cardona was the cocky type. I wouldn't be surprised if he slept with the objects. "Can your Pack spare any wolves?"

"I can ask my Alpha, but I don't think it'll be a problem. Can you ask the Brooklyn Pack?" Cas asked. He belonged to the Queens Pack.

"I can, but I'd prefer not to ask for any favors right now."

I'd already involved the Brooklyn Pack in too many of my exploits. The less I involved them now was for the best. I chose not to be part of a Pack, so I had to remember not to always run to them when I needed help.

"Now let's take a look at this stone," Briggs said as he stepped closer to us.

As everyone hovered around me, I pulled the box away from my chest and unlatched the golden lock, lifting the top. A deep purple cushion lined the inside of the box and nestled the stone on top. The rock was oval and about the size of a hockey puck. Other than that, it was just a gray rock.

"*This* is the Skofnung stone?" I said, dumbfounded and underwhelmed. "*This* is supposed to heal?"

Cas shook his head. "According to legend, it's supposed to heal any wound made by the Skofnung sword. But when the relics are combined, it's a healing agent."

"This is all super confusing," I muttered. "Where's the sword?"

Cas shrugged. "That's something I'd rather not know, and as long as no one's searching for it, it's none of my business."

I snorted. "I can literally throw this out in Central Park and it would just get lost in the array of other gray rocks. No one would ever know."

"Pretty much." Michaels brushed his finger over the uneven

surface. "Who's going to hide it? We can't keep it here in the station; it'll be the first place he checks."

"And I can't keep it," I said. "He's already gunning for me."

None of us would be good carriers of the stone. Cardona would come for anyone in the SIU. We were all targets. There was literally nowhere safe to keep it.

"I can hold on to it," Ranulf suggested from behind us. "I will give it to Alexander to carry. No one will suspect him."

That was actually pretty damn smart. It was common knowledge that I'd never risk Alexander's life. He'd be the last person anyone would think to go to. Alexander it was.

WE SENT Ranulf through a portal with a Traveler to Brooklyn in case someone was scouting the SIU. The last thing we needed was our plan falling apart at the very beginning. He complained a lot, and there was some Scottish grumbling I didn't quite understand about leaving me behind, but Cassidy promised to deliver me to Brooklyn safe and sound. It was so annoying how I needed a babysitter.

Briggs stomped into his office to do gods knew what. He wasn't thrilled about what we were planning, and I wondered if they had *him* by the proverbial balls as well. He left us to devise a plan for how to capture Cardona. We needed something stealthy that he wouldn't see coming. So far, our best plan was for me to play bait.

"He has a lot of warlocks on retainer," I mentioned as we huddled in the conference room. "I've met with him twice now, and each time he's brought multiple warlocks."

"Let's ask the witches what that's about," Michaels said, getting up to leave.

I lifted my hand to stop him. "No point in asking Belinda. There's only one person she answers to, and that's Voight," I said of the Head Witch of the SIU. Not to mention she and I didn't get along, so if I could avoid her, that would be best. "I know Briggs doesn't want us involving the Cap, but he might be supplying Cardona with warlocks. We need to plead a case to him and find a way to stop him. One of the warlocks, before I killed him," I winced, "said I had no idea what he was getting out of his deal with Cardona. That tells me they're getting something in exchange. They're not working for him for free."

"We need to set up a meeting with Voight," Finn suggested. "Without letting Briggs know."

"That's going to be tricky." Cas pressed his lips together.

"Leave it to me," Finn offered. "I'll appear to him as a Reaper and set up a place and time to meet." As a black cloud, no one would know it was him and he could get into just about anywhere without being detected. It was a solid plan.

"If we can get the warlocks on our side, whenever we set up the bait, he won't expect them to turn on him," Michaels said. "He'll be expecting the bait and be prepared for that, but he won't see the betrayal coming. This plan might work."

I nodded. "And if we get the other two objects out from under him at the same time, he *really* won't see it coming."

We ironed out the logistics before everyone left to do their part. Finn was off to see the Captain, Michaels was headed to Queens in Cassidy's place to talk to the Alpha about getting some wolves to tail Cardona, and Cas was walking me home.

As we walked along the streets of Brooklyn Heights, he spent most of the way talking about what we'd found and how we were going to move forward. I partially listened because honestly, I was exhausted. It'd been a long day for me, and I still had to deal with Sebastian when I got home. He would be all set to grill me about where I went this morning. I'd gotten away with it with Alexander and Ranulf, but it wouldn't be that easy with Bash.

The hour was late, but even the late hour couldn't disguise the balmy heat. The summer was dripping into fall with the speed of thick honey and I couldn't be happier. I didn't know how much more of this I could withstand.

"Do you need me to pick you up tomorrow?" Cas asked as we passed a street lined with brownstones.

I shook my head. "I think Ranulf is going to escort me. I should be good, but thanks." I could see our house just down the street. It was the only brownstone with the lights still on.

"We're going to get this guy, Kenz. It's not you he's after, you just got in his way. It could have easily been me, or Finn, or even Michaels."

I snorted. "I always seem to get in the way."

He gave me a sad smile. "You're an easy target."

That much was true. Everyone wanted me dead for some reason or another. It was why I couldn't fathom why Alexander still wanted me as Queen. The Lycan world would just inherit all my enemies.

"Well, here we are." Cas stopped in front of my house. "Let me know if you need anything."

"Thanks, Cas." I squeezed his upper arm and parted ways. Jogging up the steps to the front door, I unlocked it and went inside to face the music.

The house was cooler than it was outside, which meant Bash

had the A/C turned up. I dropped my things by the door as usual and headed to the living room, where I found someone I didn't expect.

I expected to find Bash watching TV, shirtless, in his pajama bottoms, barefoot, waiting impatiently for me to come home. Instead, I found Alexander seated next to the table lamp, reading a newspaper and sipping a cup of tea. That wasn't the shocking part. What had me slack jawed was that he wasn't wearing his usual suit attire that screamed royalty. He wore a pair of fashionable dark jeans, a crisp white t-shirt, and a pair of boots. He looked so casual. Young. And most importantly, really out of place.

"Am I missing something?" I muttered as I stepped further into the living room.

He lowered the top half of the newspaper and peered over at me. "Mackenzie," his voice rumbled. "There ye are. I was wondering when ye'd come home."

I frowned. "Where's Bash?"

"He went to sleep. I told him I'd stay up and wait for ye."

"Okay ..." I replied, a little confused. "I guess I should go to bed."

Alexander folded his newspaper and set it down beside him. "Sit and talk with me for a while, lass. Better yet, let's go for a walk."

My eyes widened. "At this time of night? It's two in the morning, Alexander."

He shrugged. "Two AM is when I do my best thinking." He took one last sip from his teacup before setting it down and standing from the sofa. He straightened to his full height and walked toward the door, expecting me to follow. "Come on, now."

This was completely insane, and I was equally as insane because I followed him out the door. Alexander looked so very human in his attire as he walked the streets of Brooklyn with me trailing along behind him. If the others ever saw him, they'd never believe it. He still held his head up with his nose in the air like royalty, but he walked with a swagger I didn't recognize. What was with him?

"Did Ranulf give you—"

"Quiet, Mackenzie," he cut me off. "We do not speak of such things in the open. The wind listens."

I wanted to correct him and say there was no wind because we were in the dead of summer, but I got the gist of what he was trying to say. There were ears everywhere.

"Sorry," I mumbled. "So why are we walking around the neighborhood in the middle of the night?"

He peered over his shoulder at me and grinned. "Have ye ever flown, Mackenzie?"

I jerked, taken aback. "Like on a plane?" Was he about to take me on a trip? Now was not the time.

Alexander chuckled. "No, darling. Nae a plane. Have *ye* ever flown from the sky?"

I choked on nothing but air. "Of course not! Lycan can't fly! Are you nuts?"

"We Lycan can do many things, lass. I want to show ye something. Will ye come with me?" He stopped in the middle of the sidewalk and held out a hand for me to take.

He was talking about flying. There was no way we could fly! I knew that for a fact. What was he planning? Did I trust Alexander? This was the ultimate test. His features were sincere, his face soft and welcoming, with that one black curl falling over his forehead that always reminded me of Superman. *Was* he Superman?

I placed my hand in his. I supposed I was about to find out.

Hand in hand, we walked across blocks and blocks of Brooklyn until we left Brooklyn Heights. I wondered how he knew his way around. He must have been sightseeing while I was at work. We were in a warehouse district, surrounded by buildings at least ten stories tall.

Giddy like a kid on Christmas, Alexander dragged me inside an abandoned building full of manufacturing machines. He took me to a set of stairs and started to climb. We ascended all the floors, and by the time we made it to the roof, I was sweating. We practically raced up the stairs and he hadn't let me go.

"Alexander, what is going on?" I said breathlessly.

We opened the door to the rooftop and I heard the crunch of gravel beneath our feet. Peering up, we were met with the inky darkness of the night sky. I could see how high up we were; it was the tallest building compared to the other warehouses in the area.

"How did you find this place?" I asked.

"I've been exploring Brooklyn in yer absence," he answered with a grin. "It's a wonderful place."

I snorted. "You think an abandoned warehouse is a wonderful place?"

"Look at the sky from here, Mackenzie. The stars are so clear compared to the city, where ye cannae see them at all. And we're so high, ye can almost touch them," he said dreamily.

He was right, you couldn't see the stars in the city, but I still didn't see what his fascination with this place was. It was a dump.

Without releasing my hand, Alexander led me to the edge of the roof. "Look down below."

I did, and the sight of the ground so far below us made me waver a little on my feet. I wasn't scared of heights, but we were a little too close to the edge for comfort. I'd jumped from buildings before, but those were two-story buildings, nothing this high.

"You're not going to jump ... are you?" I looked uneasily at Alexander.

His grin widened. "*We* are."

"Oh, hell no!" I exclaimed, trying to pull my hand from his grip. "We'll die!"

It finally happened. Alexander lost his marbles.

He laughed. "Where's the big, bad Mackenzie Grey?"

"Scared shitless right now." I peered over the edge again. "Is this what you meant by flying?"

He nodded. "Sometimes when I need to clear my head, this is what I come to do. And I think ye have a lot on yer mind right now, darling. Ye forget that as a wolf ye have great reflexes. Plus, yer also supernatural."

"So now I'm a damn cat?" I said dryly.

"No," he laughed. "Would ye just trust me, darling?"

Once again, he held out his hand for me to take. I hadn't realized he'd let me go. Alexander stepped up onto the edge of the roof, ready to take a leap. If I did this, I might plummet to my death. Or it could be the most exhilarating moment of my life. Who knew? All I knew right then was that I was about to shit a brick at how high we were.

"Fly with me, Mackenzie," he whispered, and a chill ran through me.

"You haven't steered me wrong yet," I mumbled and slipped

my hand in his. "I'm putting all my trust in you, Alexander." With his help, I climbed up to the edge of the roof and stood side by side with him.

"I won't let ye get hurt, darling. Never. Now close yer eyes."

I took a deep breath and exhaled. Doing as I was told, my eyes fluttered shut. My senses went into overdrive as they picked up on my current fear. I could hear the honking of cars blocks away, the warbling sirens of an ambulance miles away. My skin was sensitive and I felt the dribble of every sweat drop rolling down my skin. I could also smell the garbage left to rot in the dumpsters behind the warehouse.

"Turn around," Alexander said, and I tensed. "Trust me." I swiveled around, giving the dead air my back. "On the count of three, just let go," he whispered. "One ... two ... three ..."

Alexander took my hand and we fell backward into the air. The air whooshed around me, my hair flying all around my face, and my stomach clenched as I dropped, feeling like I was on a rollercoaster. My body locked up at first, but Alexander grabbed my hand and something transferred between us — an energy I couldn't explain or put into words — but my whole body relaxed and I felt weightless, like I was flying.

Nothing mattered in that moment. Not the case, not the fact I was expected to be Queen, not that more than half of the supernatural community was gunning for me, nothing. I was free. I spread my arms out beside me and just as a smile was spreading across my face, I landed in a cradle formed from a pair of arms. I opened my eyes to see I was in Alexander's arms and we were on solid ground.

"How?" I gasped as I looked around.

He set me down and I wobbled a little on my legs until I got my footing. "How did it feel, Mackenzie?"

I was speechless. How did I feel? I didn't know how to put it into words. I never knew it was possible to do something like that. I mean, I knew we weren't actually flying, we were just jumping, but it felt like I was flying. If he hadn't caught me, I would have been a splat on the ground because I had zoned out completely.

"When our hands touched ... what was that?" My brows furrowed.

"I'm an Alpha, lass. Ye were terrified, and I had to calm ye down. When ye take over, ye'll have this ability as well. It will pass on to my kin."

I nodded thoughtfully. "You said you do this when you need to clear your head ... and now I see why. But why show me your spot? Isn't that private?"

He smiled softly and approached me. His hands grabbed me delicately on each side of my face and he tilted me up to face him. He pressed a kiss on my forehead and pulled back without letting me go. "My darling girl, I will share everything with ye, even my last dying breath. If this can bring ye comfort in yer trying times, why would I nae show ye?"

I peered at Alexander in the eyes that matched mine and saw just how much he loved me. Even though he'd only known me a short amount of time, even though I'd caused so much trouble. He'd forgiven so much, and even then, those gray eyes looked at me with a father's unconditional love.

I swallowed the lump forming in my throat. "I want to do it again. But this time, teach me how to land."

He grinned. "Of course."

16

I was running on fumes, having spent most of the night jumping off buildings with Alexander. Even though it sounded ridiculous, it was the most relaxed I'd been in days. And it was fun. We walked into the house around six in the morning and I only got a few hours of sleep before Bash nudged me awake.

Now Ranulf and I were at the station and I was on my third cup of coffee, trying to stay alert.

"Repeat what you said again?" I groaned as I rested my head on my hand, my elbow propped on the conference table.

Finn growled, "Pay attention, Grey. *I said*," he emphasized the last portion, "I met with Voight and ... *persuaded* him into aligning with us."

I sipped on my ninety-nine-cent cup of coffee. "Persuaded? You mean you threatened," I chuckled. "What did he look like when you reaper'd him?" Ranulf smacked me in the back of the head. "Ouch!" I rubbed my scalp.

"Stupid girl," he grumbled.

Finn looked up at the ceiling and tapped his chin pensively. "He looked a little constipated. Maybe because I approached him while he was on the toilet."

I burst out laughing and smacked my palm on the table. "You didn't!"

Finn smirked. "I did."

"You're sick," Michaels grimaced.

"It's an effective negotiation technique," Finn defended himself. "I got him at his most vulnerable."

"Yeah, you did," I smirked, and Finn returned the look.

"So he was the one supplying the warlocks to Cardona?" Cas asked.

Finn nodded. "He said Cardona has a very ancient relic of theirs and is holding it hostage until this is over. You know how warlocks are with their toys. But I promised him we'd help him find it in exchange for his cooperation, or else he was going down with Cardona."

Good. I was trying not to imagine the Captain being accosted by a cloud of black smoke while he was on the shitter. Definitely not a good look for anyone. But as long as he was on our side and we had the warlocks in check, our plan was a go.

"What about the wolves?" I asked, turning to Michaels.

"The Alpha for the Queens Pack lent us two of his best trackers. I already have them out on the street tailing Cardona and reporting his movements. We should have a detailed report by this evening," Michaels said in his gruff New York accent.

"Excellent." I sipped on my coffee. "Now what about the rest of the plan?"

"I've been thinking about that," Cas said. "We're obviously

going to use you as bait, along with the box the stone came in, just without the actual stone inside. We'll even get some random rock from the street and chuck it in there just in case. But there's nothing we can do that won't be apparent it's a trap, so we do the opposite. We contact Cardona and offer a trade."

I frowned. "Say what now?"

"You can't be serious, Chang!" Michaels leaned forward on the table. Finn kept quiet.

"Just hear me out. We tell him Grey's been attacked too much by those who wish to collect the bounty, so in exchange for him cancelling the bounty, we'll give him what he wants—the stone." Cas crossed his big arms over his chest. "He might suspect it's a trap, but he'll think twice about it because there's a level of truth to it. And he won't risk the possibility that we might actually trade the stone for Grey's safety."

"Hm ..." Finn thought about it. "And because he'll know it's a possible trap, he'll double up on warlocks for precaution. This could work."

It wasn't a bad plan. There were holes in it, sure – but none we couldn't easily cover up. It was pretty solid, and our best chance at catching Cardona. We had to take it.

"Let's do it."

―――――

I WAS at my desk working on some reports and trying to get ahold of Maximos. Unfortunately, he wasn't answering our calls and I still hadn't figured out what his link to Cardona was. Something bothered me about the whole situation. Maximos had always had a connection within the police force that cleared him every time he brushed against the law, and we always assumed it was within the SIU. But what if it wasn't? What if it was Cardona? And if it was, why would Cardona steal from a friend? These were all theories, and I wanted to get to the bottom of it by speaking to the bar owner as soon as possible, but it was almost as if he'd disappeared. I decided to run by The Third Eye myself.

Cassidy was out, checking in with the wolves, and Finn was gods knew where. Ranulf left for a meeting with Alexander back in Brooklyn, though he made me promise not to leave the station until he returned. It was just me and Michaels doing paperwork, with a few other detectives milling around the squad room. I hated to leave Michaels alone, but I had to follow my gut.

I stood and ducked down to grab my bag from beneath my desk. In that moment, a sharp ache started in my abdomen. It felt as if someone had just punched me in the gut and I hunched over automatically, groaning. I held onto my stomach for fear I was about to vomit when the pain struck again. This time it was so severe, I dropped to one knee and let out a gritted shriek.

"Grey!" Michaels dropped his papers and met me down on the ground. "What's wrong? What hurts?"

Sweat beaded on my face and my breath came out heavily. I didn't know how to explain what I was feeling. It was like someone was ripping out one of my ribs.

"Ahh!" I clutched the edge of my desk and gasped as the pain hit me again. My wolf awoke and my eyes silvered.

"Grey ... your eyes." Michaels backed up a little.

My wolf started to whine and I realized she was feeling the pain as well. It had been a while since she'd awakened on her own, which meant something was very wrong.

What's wrong, girl? I internally asked.

The bond! she cried.

I wrapped my arms around my abdomen and rocked back and forth. *Sebastian.* Something was wrong with Bash.

How could it cripple me like this? Was he feeling the same debilitating pain?

My gaze whipped up and scanned the squad room as other detectives stood around watching us. "I need ... Cas." I swallowed the lump in my throat. "Hurry!"

Michaels didn't hesitate. He shot up from the floor and hustled out of the room, leaving me crouched in a puddle of agony.

I bit down on my lip as I let the pain course through me, trying not to scream. It felt like hours until Michaels returned with Cas, who gingerly picked me up immediately.

"Mackenzie," he said quietly. "Hang in there." I didn't know where he was taking me, but I clung to him as tightly as possible, gripping his shirt and refusing to let go.

"It's ... Bash," I muttered. "He's ... hurting."

Cas nodded. "I just got the call from my Alpha. He's been taken. I was just coming to get you when Michaels found me. We need to get you to Belinda so she can reduce the pain. You won't be able to function, otherwise."

I dimly heard the ding of the elevator, but my eyes stayed tightly clenched. My head lolled against Cas's chest as he moved. When we got to the witches' station, I was placed on a gurney. I could hear the Head Witch's voice from a mile away.

"What happened, Cassidy?" Belinda asked as a flashlight shined in my eyes.

"She's feeling her Anam's pain, or distress, or, I really don't know how it works," Cas rambled. "Sebastian Steel was taken from the Brooklyn Pack's Compound not long ago. Can you ease her pain?"

"I don't know if I can. Your best bet is finding Mr. Steel," she answered as she checked my pulse.

Cas sucked his teeth. "*She's* our best bet at finding him, using their bond!" I imagined him pointing at me. Now he understood my frustrations with Belinda. I wished Amara hadn't betrayed me during the Freedom Wars and been killed. If not, she would have still been the Head Witch around here.

I attempted to sit up on the gurney, but someone pushed me back down and I collapsed. "I have … to … get to him." No matter how much I hurt, he was hurting more. I had to find him.

"I'll find him, Kenz. I promise," Cas whispered.

I shook my head. "No. I'm … coming with you." I sat up again, leaning on my forearms and blinking a couple times to focus my vision. "I have to."

Belinda sighed. "I can't give you anything for the pain. Nothing is powerful enough for an Anam bond, but I can give you a stamina potion if you're that mule-headed and insist on going."

"Give it to me," I gasped.

"Very well," she sniffed, walking back to her workstation.

The pain didn't subside, but it was almost like my body was getting used to it. I was able to move a little better, but it was still incapacitating. I just had to be careful or else we'd both be dead.

When Belinda returned, I was sitting on the gurney with my legs hanging over the edge, shivering.

"This will only help for a limited time, so find him fast," Belinda warned, handing me a vial of red potion. It looked like Kool-Aid, but I knew better.

"Bottoms up, Grey," Cas said as I took the bottle from the witch.

In one fell swoop, I took the drink in one swig and swallowed. At least it was fruity and didn't have a bad aftertaste.

I felt the effects almost immediately. My eyes widened and I shot up from the gurney. The pain was there, but it was almost like background noise.

"Oh, hell yeah!" I crowed as I shook out my arms. "I could get used to this." I felt like I'd been injected with a shot of adrenaline.

"Don't," Belinda said dryly. "I only use that for emergencies. Now hurry, you're on a timeline."

CASSIDY AND I left the SIU. As soon as I stepped outside, I closed my eyes and tuned into my wolf. I'd never intentionally tracked Bash this way before, though when I came back from Scotland and was trying to keep my distance from everyone, I would always find myself standing across the street from the warehouse in Brooklyn. It was the bond leading me to him. Now, I just needed to find a way to have it lead me to him again.

I tapped into that warm feeling inside me, the part that felt like home, and latched onto it like a tether. I opened my eyes, knowing they were silver and started to walk, following that invisible rope. Cas followed silently behind me, trusting I would lead him in the right direction.

The tug led us all around the city for almost an hour, and for a moment, I thought I was just walking around aimlessly and there was nothing actually leading us, but then I felt the warmth inside me get hotter, like a signal that I was getting closer. Once we passed the Grand Bazaar—New York City's indoor/outdoor, year-round flea market—I knew exactly where we were going. Without following the tether anymore, I headed for the Seventy-ninth Street transverse entrance to Central Park.

"They're in Central Park?" Cas asked as he trailed behind me, trying to keep up with my quick steps.

"I don't know how he did it, but I'm almost positive they're in the fae realm," I answered as we jogged through the park and headed for the lake that heralded the entrance to the realm.

Cas grabbed my arm to stop me and we skidded to a halt. "We need to inform the team. We also need to get Malakai to open the realm. Slow down, Kenz."

I shrugged off his hand. "No time. Remember? I can get in."

He grabbed for me again. "We need back-up, Grey. *Think* for a minute!"

"I *am* thinking!" I shouted. "I feel him, Cas! I need to get to him *now!*" I said with so much desperation, I thought I would start crying right in front of him. But I wouldn't. I was stronger than that.

"Just ... just let me call the team, Grey. Please." Cas released me tentatively and turned for some privacy to pull out his cell phone and call the others.

I could have just left. I would have. The old Mackenzie would have. But if I did, it would just take them longer to reach me because they'd have to wait for Malakai to open the fae realm for them. By then, both Bash and I could be dead. There was no point ditching him now, no matter how badly every cell in my body wanted to. Cas was right, I needed the team to back me up. I might be juiced up on that stamina potion, but I still felt the pain of the bond in the furthest edges of my mind. Whenever the potion's effects finally wore off, I'd feel everything all over again.

"The team is on their way and they're bringing Malakai with them, so we can go ahead without them." With Cas's words, I didn't wait a second more. I hurried into the park and headed straight for the lake. I pushed past humans, not caring if I bumped into them or not as long as I got to my destination.

When we arrived at the lake, I stepped to the edge and placed my hand on top of the water, feeling the ripple beneath me. The water spread apart like the Red Sea and made a pathway for me and Cas. At the far end was a waterfall that shimmered with iridescent rainbows. Cas and I hurried between the two walls of water until we reached the end and walked straight into the waterfall. Not a single droplet landed on us as we emerged into the brightness of the fae realm.

The warmth in my abdomen was on fire now and I knew we were close.

"He's here." I swiveled around the green pasture, wondering where to go. "I just don't know where."

"They won't be in the woods." Cas shook his head in deep thought. "Without a fae guide, it's too easy to get lost."

"They must have one. How else would they have gotten here?" I said, hysteria in my voice. I should have just given the fae what they wanted. "What if it was the fae who took him, and not Cardona?"

"No. The fae wouldn't start another war with the Lycan. They're not that stupid."

"If they helped Cardona kidnap Sebastian, they're well on their way to starting another war!" I yelled into the vastness. The minute they took Bash, they declared war. I would never forgive them.

A buzzing sound came from the forest. It was far away, but getting louder by the second.

"What is that?" I mumbled as I turned in the direction of the woods.

Cas placed his arm in front of me and pushed me behind him. "I don't know, but it sounds like it's coming toward us fast." Cassidy growled as he went into a half shift and crouched in front of me in a protective stance.

The bushes rattled before a little ball of light came bursting out of them. Cas straightened when a pixie emerged. As it got closer, we realized it was Nyx, the pixie who guided us through the forest last time.

"Queen Slayer." She buzzed in front of our faces, her hands on her hips as she floated before us. "It's about time you got here."

I frowned. "What are you talking about?"

"The Alpha of the Brooklyn Pack is here, but he won't last much longer," she said as she flew in an agitated circle around us. "You *are* here to rescue him, aren't you?"

I pushed past Cas. "Where is he?" I growled.

"Touchy, touchy," she squeaked. "Follow me." She buzzed away and we had to run to keep up. Instead of going into the woods, she flew in the opposite direction, going down a path made of clear glass that zig-zagged across a green pasture that suddenly felt very familiar. This was the same general path Ranulf and I had taken through the forest when we tried to enter the Queen's castle.

"Are you taking us to the glass castle?" I asked, because this wasn't exactly the way I remembered Ranulf and I taking. Then again, we didn't have the luxury of a fae guide back then.

"Not exactly," Nyx said over her shoulder. "I'm taking you to the dungeons. It's where they're holding your Alpha."

"Hold on a minute!" Cas stopped us and it took Nyx a moment before she realized we'd stopped running.

"We don't have much time, Queen Slayer."

"You said the dungeons, as in the Queen's dungeons?" Cas asked.

She nodded. "Correct."

Cas snarled. "Rumor has it, those dungeons are laced with silver. Are you walking us into a trap?"

Never trust a fae. That should have been obvious. I was so desperate to help Bash, I completely overlooked the fact that Nyx could be walking us into a bloodbath. I needed to be more objective, but my emotions were scattered everywhere. All I could think about was getting to Bash, no matter what.

I snatched Nyx from the air and gripped her in my palm. "You better start talking, pixie," I growled.

She whined as she wriggled to free herself from my grasp; it felt like a caterpillar tickling my hand. "I swear it's not a trick, Queen Slayer!" she cried. "There is silver in the dungeons, but that is where your Alpha is. I do not lie!"

"We need to wait for the others, Grey. Neither of us can go down there," Cas relented.

"No!" I let Nyx go. "Lead us to the dungeons. I'll go down by myself."

The pixie shook herself off indignantly and started to fly in the direction we needed to go, but Cas stopped me from following by grabbing my arm.

"Are you insane?" he muttered. "Sebastian is probably passed out from the silver, and you won't get past the first cell. We can't take that risk."

I ripped my arm away. "I'm not leaving him down there for one more second!" I seethed. "I'm going, and that's final. You can wait for the others."

Without waiting for his response, I followed Nyx and ran to catch up.

17

The meandering road led us to the Queen's glass castle. What was once a vibrant, shining home was now dim and full of cobwebs. It was evident that no one had lived there in a long time. Once she passed, the fae abandoned it.

Instead of going through the front door, we went around to the back of the glass castle where there was an underground entrance that looked like a tornado shelter. Cassidy opened the wooden double doors, but Nyx stopped him from going further.

"Once you go down these steps, the silver will hit you," she said. "Do with that as you please."

Both Cas and I peered down at the entrance. It was pitch black, except for a flickering lantern situated at the far bottom. It was a long way down. If the silver hit while we were going down the stairs, we could easily fall.

"Rethink this, Kenz," Cas murmured. "We can always wait for back-up."

"No. I'm not waiting. He needs me now." I looked into the

abyss once again and had an idea. "I promise we'll make it out, Cas." I looked at him and grinned. "You can't get rid of me that easily."

He rolled his eyes. "As if I could."

I took a couple steps back and waved him back as well. "I need some space." He moved out of the way, as did Nyx.

"What are you going to do—"

I didn't respond. I gave myself a running head start before jumping into the gaping hole of darkness. The whoosh of air blew across my face, whipping my hair as I held my arms out beside me and slightly bent my legs for landing. The small drop in my gut receded and I relaxed into the fall. I looked down at the lantern to gauge when I was getting close to the ground, and then suddenly, I was crouching on the ground, landing perfectly with only a slight vibration rattling through my bones from the force of the land.

"Kenzie!" Cassidy whisper-shouted.

"I'm okay!" I shouted back.

"You're officially insane! You nearly gave me a heart attack!"

I chuckled and took the lantern that hung on the wall. "I'll be back."

After only a couple steps into the damp, concrete tunnel, I started to wobble. A sleepiness took over me and I stumbled to the side, falling against the concrete wall to prop myself up. *The silver.*

I jumped the staircase to prevent the silver from getting me while I was going down the stairs, but it wasn't until you started walking into the tunnel that you started feeling the effects.

I shook my head a couple times to clear my vision and stumbled forward while holding myself up by the wall. I had to stay alert—I had to stay awake. I'd never felt this way from silver before. What were the fae doing with so much silver? Or what had *Drusilla* been doing with so much silver?

The tunnel finally opened to a room full of cells on either side of the narrow walkway. I grabbed the first cell bar I saw to hold myself up, but as soon as I touched it, it burned through my flesh and I screamed.

"Ah!" I dropped to the ground, the lantern rolling away with a clatter as I clutched my burned hand to my chest.

"Mackenzie?" someone garbled.

From where I perched on my knees, I looked up and saw a figure at the end of the row of cells. It was so dark I couldn't make out who it was, even with my wolf vision.

With my only functional hand, I reached for the lantern that had rolled away, but I was so weak, I wanted nothing more than to stay on the ground. I pushed myself to stand and dragged myself forward, aiming the light toward the stranger. When I got close enough, I held the light up to their face.

Sebastian!

He was chained, hanging from the ceiling, being held up by his neck with the tips of his toes barely brushing the floor, which was why I didn't recognize his voice when he called out my name. This was why I was in such pain. He was surrounded by mountains of silver and was barely holding on.

"Bash!" I reached for the chains that restrained him.

"No!" he choked, stopping me. "Pure ... silver."

My brows furrowed. I didn't understand what that meant. "Is that what burned me?" I asked, hating that I was making him talk.

"Yes," he garbled.

I wavered on my feet as if I were about to faint and sweat started rolling down the side of my face. It was taking a lot of energy from me to stay alert.

"I can't *not* try to help you," I whispered because it was all the strength I had. "I don't care if it burns. You're hurting."

"Run," he choked.

It was all the warning I had before I whipped around and came face-to-face with someone—species unknown—taking advantage of my weakness. They yanked my hair and I blocked their arm with my forearm, palming their chest with as much strength as I could muster. They flew back a couple of feet, but I was already gasping for breath. That small skirmish took a lot out of me.

Once the torches in the dungeon were lit by a warlock at the end of the room, I could see everyone that surrounded us more clearly.

"Ms. Grey, welcome," Cardona greeted smoothly as he stood in the center, surrounded by his beefy protection detail. "I see you got my message."

"Release him," I demanded breathlessly as I pointed to Bash.

Cardona shrugged. "I'd be happy to do so, as long as you cooperate."

"He's dying!" I gasped. "If you want me to cooperate, let him go *now!*"

He tsked. "That's not how negotiations work. You, of all people should know that. You're practically an expert at them with how you handled your re-employment."

I collapsed to a knee, unable to hold myself up any longer. I fisted the ground and took in shallow breaths. Cassidy was right, I couldn't last much longer. I didn't expect them to have pure silver down there. Hell, I didn't even know about pure silver or the effects of it. What the hell kind of silver had I been dealing with before this?

"You won't get the stone unless you release him. That's how *this* negotiation works," I mumbled. "I have nothing to lose. I'm dying right along with him, and no one else knows where it is. If I die, the stone will be lost forever," I bluffed. He didn't know Alexander had it, and it was best if he thought the rest of the SIU team didn't know where it was, either.

Cardona sneered at me before jerking his head at one of the fae standing beside him. "Release him," he said none too happily.

I recognized the white-haired fae that approached us as the one who walked out of the portal and made the offer to bestow some great power on me. He claimed they only wished to keep me safe, but from my current vantage point, it certainly didn't look that way.

The fae passed by and stood just behind me, unchaining Bash. I took the opportunity to chat him up. If he really wanted to help, this was his chance.

"Psst." I tried to get his attention without gaining the attention of the others. "Hey!"

The fae with those eerie lavender eyes peered down at me, looked over at Cardona, and back down at me again. "What do you want, Mackenzie MacCoinnich?"

"That's the question I should be asking you," I mumbled. "What do you want from me? I'll give it to you, just help us," I begged.

"I once offered my help and you denied me. Why should I help you now?" He tilted his head as if I truly confounded him.

"I'm not a good liar, so you'll get the truth from me. I don't trust you. I don't trust any of the fae." I breathed deeply. "But right now, I'm in a bit of a pickle, and I don't plan on dying here."

The fae squatted down to be at eye level with me. "One vial."

"What?" I scoffed.

"One vial of your blood. It's all I ask."

What the fuck kinda kinky shit was this? Did the oxygen completely leave my brain, or did I hear him correctly?

"That's not what you wanted originally," I muttered, trying to keep myself from laying on the ground. I wanted to fall asleep, but I couldn't. I tried to focus on the pain from the burnt hand I still clutched to my chest.

"How do you know that wasn't what I wanted?" He raised a brow.

"Because you said—"

"I wanted to bestow upon you great powers. I know what I said, Mackenzie MacCoinnich. No need to repeat my words. Now hurry and make a decision. We are running out of time." He peered over at Cardona and started to unchain Bash.

"What's the hold-up?" the Commissioner yelled across the room.

"Almost done," the fae called back. "Clock's ticking, Mackenzie MacCoinnich. What have you decided?"

I looked back at Bash, who took a deep breath as soon as the chains around his neck were released. He dropped to the ground when the ones holding him up were untied and he started to cough. All I wanted to do was go to him. Through our bond, I felt his pain subside and my body visibly relaxed. But there was a nasty burn mark around his neck where the chains of pure silver had been.

"I'll do it," I said to the fae. "I'll give you the vial. Just get rid of Cardona."

A slow smile spread across the fae's face. "As you wish, Mackenzie MacCoinnich."

His lavender eyes glowed as he stepped over us and magic pulsed through his body. He spread his hands out beside him and I felt the magic swell around us. The ground beneath us started to crack, and in those splits of earth, green vines started to sprout. They darted out of the earth and found their way to Cardona, wrapping themselves around his body and clutching him tightly.

"What is the meaning of this, Angus?" Cardona yelled as he was restrained by the vines.

I crawled over to Bash and wrapped my arms around him protectively. "Are you okay?" I whispered.

He nodded his head but didn't say anything.

"The terms of our conditions have been nullified," the fae whom I now knew was named Angus said as he approached the Commissioner. "I now have what I want."

The fae that were spread around the room released knives from their sleeves and stepped up behind the warlocks, intending to slit their throats.

"Stop!" I shouted. "Don't kill them!"

Angus lifted a hand to stop them, and the fae restrained the warlocks to stop them from doing any magic. I exhaled raggedly, having already exerted more energy than I contained. We'd promised the Captain no more warlocks would die and I intended to keep that promise.

I heard footsteps coming from the tunnel and sighed in relief, fully expecting someone from my team. But I should have known I wasn't that lucky.

Captain Voight appeared in the dungeon, standing just behind Cardona, and for a moment I thought he was there to help us. Until he held up two fingers and pointed them in Angus's direction. The fae seized before me, the lavender glow in his eyes fading before he was flung back against the concrete wall behind us. Debris rained down from the impact as Angus collapsed and was knocked out. Once Angus was unconscious, the power that held the vines restraining Cardona were released.

Voight walked down the aisle and glanced at the fae holding his warlocks hostage, then raised his hands and brought them down forcefully, sending a vibration radiating through the dungeon. The fae were thrown back against the wall and rendered as unconscious as their leader.

"You played us ..." I accused Voight as I looked around the room with wide eyes.

He stopped mid-way to me and straightened. "I'm the High Warlock of Long Island. I do not fear a Reaper," he said disgustedly.

We underestimated him. He may have been scared in the moment, but that fear faded.

I looked down at Bash in my arms and saw he was too weak to fight. Hell, *I* was too weak to fight. There was no chance of us getting out of there. Where were the others?

The question must have been obvious on my face, because Voight laughed. "Your friends are a bit occupied. Don't expect them to come save you anytime soon."

I glowered. "What did you do to them?"

"Nothing that concerns you, Grey," Voight said. "Now, give us the stone so we can get on with our day."

Why wasn't Úlfur coming to save the day? When did I

become so reliant on the stranger that I even expected him to show up?

No. I needed to figure this out on my own. There were four warlocks in addition to Voight, and then there was Cardona. I had to find a way out for Bash and me. I'd been given a stamina potion, which was probably why I was more lucid than Bash and had more energy. I could get to my feet and do a half shift. The real question was, could I fight?

I wavered and attempted to stand, and once I was on my feet, stumbled until I got my footing. The room was spinning and I tried to focus on a stationary point in the room to get it to stop.

I gave them an overconfident smirk, even if I didn't actually feel it. "I seem to always get underestimated. When will you learn? I don't deal well with ultimatums."

"The room is laced with pure silver, Grey. You're smarter than that," Voight chided as if talking to a child. "Let's not do anything stupid."

I laughed. "You kidnap my soon-to-be mate to lure me to the fae realm, and then tell me not to do anything stupid? You're the definition of stupid!" I roared and morphed into a half shift, my canines emerging and my claws coming out. My eyes silvered and I growled at my enemies, getting a boost of energy from their spike of fear. "You came for what's mine ... *now you'll pay!*"

I launched myself toward the first warlock, my claws slashing across his face so he couldn't see. He screamed and held the ribbons of his face as blood streamed down like a river. Not about to give him a chance to do any magic, I snapped his neck. By the time I spun around, the others were ready. As they heaved magic balls at me, each one bounced off my skin like I was wearing warlock repellent. I didn't know if it was the stamina potion or not, but I no longer felt the physical effects of the impact. I just kept walking toward them.

Two came for me at once. I ducked a hit and punched him in the gut while blocking the other warlock, who tried to grab me before I twisted his arm and flipped him on his back. I elbowed the other warlock in the face, making blood spurt from his nose. The third one joined the fray and I tackled him to the ground, straddling him and letting my punches fly until I knocked him out cold.

I was hauled off by the one I'd flipped onto his back and he wrapped his arms around me, pinning my arms to my sides. I head-butted him until he let me go, making myself dizzy in the process. When he released me, I turned and sank my canines into his throat and ripped it out. His blood flowed from my mouth, down my chin and neck, and I felt the bloodlust frenzy take over. I wanted more. Two warlocks remained. One was unconscious, but the other was starting to retreat, placing himself in a magical quarantine to keep me away.

My gaze went to Voight and Cardona, who were rooted in place, transfixed by the spectacle. "You!" I pointed to Voight. "I will kill you ..."

"You do that, and your career is over!"

I chuckled dryly. "*Your* career is over. Both of you are dead for touching something that didn't belong to you," I growled.

"Mackenzie ..." Bash croaked from behind me, but his voice sounded so far away. "Please ... control yourself."

"You might want to listen to your boyfriend," Voight snapped as he erected a magical barrier between us.

I snarled at him like a feral animal, approaching the magical barrier and pounding on it. "You can't hide from me forever!"

"Grey?" The voice came from behind them, and when I looked, I saw Michaels. Luckily, he wasn't alone. Finn and Malakai were with him.

My chest was heaving up and down rapidly, but as soon as I saw my partner, something inside of me realized I was doing something I shouldn't. Something inhuman. I calmed immediately and looked down at my bloody hands and shirt, stumbling back from the magical barrier in mild shock.

Michaels came around to me and wrapped me in his arms. "It's okay, just breathe."

I shook my head and stepped away. I had to get to Bash. I didn't have time for a breakdown now. "I have to get Bash out of here," I muttered, trying to avoid looking at the massacre I'd inflicted.

"I'll help you." Michaels and I approached Sebastian where he laid on the floor and picked him up. Michaels took most of his weight, since I was coming down from an adrenaline high and the silver was starting to affect me again. I could feel myself dragging.

I peered over at Cardona and Voight as Malakai brought down their magical barrier and Finn swooped in with handcuffs for them both. Focusing on the task at hand, I didn't bother looking back or seeing what was happening with the others as I stumbled out of the dungeons with Michaels and Bash. We trudged up the stairs until we were outside, where we were greeted by an armada.

Cassidy and Nyx weren't the only ones waiting on us. So were the Captains of the Brooklyn Pack, here to retrieve their Alpha. As soon as he emerged, they hurried to his side and took him from me and Michaels, placing him as far away from the dungeon's entrance as possible.

Michaels gave me a concerned look. "I need to go back down there and arrest the other warlocks. Will you be okay?"

I nodded. He was hesitant but left me to go do his job.

Cas was by my side immediately. "Damnit, Kenz, you had me freaking out."

"Sorry," I mumbled.

"Kenz!" someone shouted, and I whirled around to see who it was.

I couldn't believe my eyes. "Ollie?" I said, confused to see him in the fae realm.

He picked me up in a massive hug, disregarding the fact I was getting blood all over him. "I've been so worried," he muttered into my hair. "I wouldn't let them come without me. I had to know you were okay."

Well, that explains why he's here.

I started to pull back but he gripped my arms, not letting go. "You shouldn't have come, Ollie. It's dangerous here, and you're not properly trained—"

"I wasn't going to leave you alone," he interrupted me. "The Brooklyn Pack was coming for Bash, but I knew none of them would be there for you."

That wasn't necessarily true; I had my team from the SIU, but I got the gist of what he was saying. At least I knew that whether he was Pack or not, my brother would always have my back, no matter what.

"Thank you, Ollie." I wrapped my arms around his waist, resting my head on his chest. He was family, no matter what our DNA said.

"Hey, Kenz, you okay?" Jackson asked as he approached us.

I stepped back and plastered on a fake smile. "Yeah, I'm fine. How's Bash?"

"He just needs to shift, but we want to do it away from *here*," he said disgustedly. "We need to get him back home. It'll be safe for him to shift in Central Park." Jackson peered over his shoulder at his Alpha. Bernard, Thomas, Mohammad, and Sterling were lifting Bash up, getting ready to transport him out of the fae realm. "We'll take care of him." Jack turned back to me, giving me a knowing look. "Just come home soon."

I nodded. "I will."

Jackson turned to Ollie and my brother shook his head. "I'm staying with Kenzie."

I placed a hand on my brother's arm. "I'll make sure he gets home to the Compound safely," I promised.

"Make sure he does, Kenz." Jackson gave Ollie a stern look and then turned away to help the other captains. It was nice to see Sterling with them. She was finally one of them.

Once they were gone, Cas, Ollie, and I waited outside the dungeon entrance until Finn, Malakai, and Michaels emerged with Cardona and Voight, as well as the other warlocks who hadn't been killed. We were three Lycans who couldn't be down there to help, even if we wanted to.

By the time they finally surfaced, back-up had arrived in the form of more officers from the SIU who were there to help take them into custody, led by Nyx. Finn, Michaels, and Malakai were also able to rescue the fae who were down there. I told them how they had tried to help, but that Voight did a whammy on them and knocked them out. Malakai was able to wake them up with some fae magic, and I approached Angus, who was propped up against the glass castle.

I squatted down in front of him. "How are you feeling?"

He rubbed his forehead and grinned. "None too pleased at the moment. Suffice it to say that you have eliminated our enemy?" Angus's eyes raked over my blood-soaked clothing.

I grimaced. "Not exactly. We took them into custody and they'll be going to Ironwood for a very long time. At least Voight will. Cardona will most likely go to a human prison."

He narrowed his lavender eyes. "That is not justice, Mackenzie MacCoinnich. At least not *your* brand of justice."

I winced. "I'm trying to do things a little differently now." *At least when the blood lust doesn't take over.*

"Your savagery is what makes you infamous—"

"It's what makes me dangerous," I cut him off. "I won't kill unnecessarily. Not anymore."

He eyed me for a moment before nodding. "Very well. As for our deal, you still owe me a vial. I will be coming to collect soon." When Angus pushed up from the ground and stood, I followed. He whistled, getting the attention of the other fae who had accompanied him, and opened a portal. "Until we meet again, Mackenzie MacCoinnich."

Then they were gone.

18

After getting patched up by a very grumpy Belinda, I was back in the squad's conference room where the team was meeting with Briggs to deliver a briefing on what happened during our mission to the fae realm. It hadn't necessarily been sanctioned.

Malakai raised his hands across the table. "I'm just the fae liaison. I had nothing to do with this. My job was merely to open the realm for your team," he said, effectively washing his hands of the situation.

I rolled my eyes at him. "Puh-leaze." I turned my attention to Briggs, who sat at the head of the table, fuming. "Listen, boss, if anyone should be taking the heat for this, it's me. Sebastian is my Anam, and I was suffering at the time. I had no choice but to go find him. And I'm glad I did, because we got those fuckers. Voight and Cardona are now locked up, as they should be."

"And where are the objects now?" Briggs barked. "You sent two Queens Pack members to trail Cardona to his home, and we've been all over that place with no success. When we asked Cardona where the relics were, the place he indicated was empty. You did a half-assed job!"

"We have the stone," Cas added from beside me. "We'll find the ring and the necklace."

"You better!" Briggs shouted, his face turning bright red. "I have Maximos calling me nonstop about his damn ring!"

I half stood from my seat. "You've been able to get ahold of Maximos?" I said a little too excitedly. I'd been trying to call him for a while now with no success. "He won't answer my calls."

"Do you think the warlocks took the objects as insurance?" Michaels suggested, which wasn't a farfetched idea. It was definitely a possibility. We still hadn't learned what it was that Cardona had of theirs.

"I don't want this case closed until those items are found!" Briggs yelled right before he stomped out of the room, slamming the glass door behind him and making it rattle.

"Yes sir." Finn saluted him, but he was already gone.

We spoke amongst ourselves, speculating about where the objects were and with whom. It was odd that they'd suddenly disappeared. We'd used compulsion on Cardona when we asked him where they were, so we knew he was telling the truth. But when we went to his penthouse in the city and searched the secret vault behind a bookshelf (shocker), there was nothing there besides human treasures. Someone beat us to it.

"It's been a long day," Cas said. "We'll continue searching tomorrow with clear heads."

"Yeah," I sighed, thinking of Ollie sitting at my desk, waiting for me to get off work so he could go home. "I need to get back to Brooklyn."

"You need one of us to take you home?" Finn offered.

I laughed. "I think the danger is gone. Anyway, I'll be chaperoned by my brother, so I should be fine. But we do need to get that bounty off the black market, ASAP."

"I already have the cyber unit working on it," Michaels said. "Should be gone by morning."

I stood from the table and walked toward the door. "Then I guess I'll see you guys tomorrow. Thanks for having my back."

"Always, Grey."

OLLIE and I made it back to Brooklyn in one piece. I kept looking over my shoulder and in dark corners, expecting something to come out and grab us, but that was just my paranoia talking. These past few days had really spiked it up. The last thing I wanted was to get my brother mixed up in all my troubles. He already felt the need to protect me.

"Are you sure you're okay?" he asked.

"For the hundredth time, I'm fine, Ollie," I chuckled. "I was a little weak from the silver and banged up from the fight, but I'm better now. Nothing for you to worry about. Just go to the Compound and check in. I'll wait for you out here, and then we can walk home together."

He watched me like he didn't really believe me, but he didn't argue. "I won't be long." Ollie hurried into the Compound and I leaned against the fence facing the sidewalk to wait for him. I would have gone inside, but I wasn't in the mood to deal with anyone right now. And if anyone else asked me if I was okay, I might explode.

"Well, I see you made it out in one piece," a voice said from down the block.

I quickly straightened to see who it was. "Úlfur." He wore his typical, impeccably-tailored suit, looking like he was out for a casual stroll with one hand lounging in his pocket. "Nice of you to show up, now that I don't need you."

He smirked and quirked a brow. "Expected me some other time?"

My hands fisted and clenched tightly. It was evident he knew when I expected him, and that I was in trouble and he didn't show. What kind of game was he playing? "You know when," I growled.

Úlfur smiled mischievously. "I could not be in two places at once, little wolf. Some things are just more important."

"And what was more important than my life?" I shouted angrily.

He shrugged one shoulder. "The relics, of course."

I gasped. It all made sense now. "*You're* the one who stole them, aren't you?" I whispered as if the others could hear, but we were the only ones on the street.

While we were tracking Cardona, and Cardona was hunting us for the stone, Úlfur was bypassing us all and stealing the ring and necklace.

"No hard feelings, little wolf," he granted as he folded the sleeves of his white button-up shirt. "I will be needing the stone."

I snorted. "Not a chance in hell."

He grinned. "I figured you'd say that. Now, I could certainly kill you for it, but I know it is not in your possession. So tell me, little wolf, who has the stone?" He finished folding his sleeves and stared at me.

"You're just going to have to kill me, because I'm not telling you a thing."

We watched each other for a few tense moments, and I could tell he was taking in every aspect and cataloging my strengths and weaknesses before attacking. Just as I thought he was about to make a move, the door to the Compound opened. My gaze snapped over to see Ollie step out and my eyes widened for fear of what was about to happen. I looked back in Úlfur's direction, but he was gone. The street was empty.

How the hell?

"You okay, sis? You look like you've seen a ghost," Ollie joked.

I grabbed his arm to steady myself and my racing heart. *He disappeared so fast! He doesn't want anyone to see him besides me. Why is that?*

"Let's go home," I muttered, and then speed-walked the two blocks it took to get to the house. I opened the door quickly and pushed Ollie in, slamming the door and locking it behind us. I knew my brother probably thought I was crazy, and after the day we had, it made sense, but it wasn't for the reasons he thought. Úlfur wanted that stone and would do whatever it took to get it.

We headed into the living room where Sebastian, Alexander, and Ranulf awaited us. I lunged for Bash immediately, who jumped up from the sofa and met me halfway, wrapping his arms around me. He must have already shifted, because he looked brand new. I hadn't had time to shift yet. Belinda gave me some tonics to speed the healing, but I wasn't at one hundred percent.

"I was so scared," I mumbled.

"I was too," he said and brushed my hair. "Thank you for coming for me."

I slapped his chest and pulled back. "Of course I'd come for you! I would never leave you to suffer." I turned around to Ranulf, knowing I owed him an apology. "I know you told me to stay put, but I couldn't do it. I hope you understand."

He grumbled something I couldn't make out, then added more clearly, "I've learned to expect ye nae to listen to me."

"I'm glad yer okay, darling." Alexander pulled me into an embrace. "Sebastian told us what ye did. To withstand pure silver!" He blew out a breath. "It's incredible."

I scratched the back of my head shyly. "I had some help."

"Nonetheless, ye are quite remarkable." Alexander squeezed me as if he couldn't be prouder. I didn't want to take all the credit. I had help from the stamina potion and they knew that, but it didn't matter to them. "Now that yer safe, it is time for me to head home and prepare for yer arrival."

I saw this coming. I knew he was only waiting until this situation cleared up to leave, but I didn't want him to leave while I had a target on my back. "When am I expected in Scotland?" He said I had to assume the throne in six months, which meant I had to come sooner than that.

"Three months from now. It's the most I can give you," he said apologetically. "I wish it could be more, darling, but time is of the essence."

I nodded and bit my lip. "Will you take the stone with you?"

"Of course, lass. It will be safe under my care." Alexander stepped away and clapped Ranulf on the back. "I think it is time we retire for the night. We'll stay for two more days so I can spend some time with ye, and then we must go. Have a good night, darling."

Alexander and Ranulf left the living room, leaving just Bash, Ollie, and me. My brother had been leaning on the wall in the far back, trying to stay out of the way. I knew he'd have to move into the Compound soon, but I was prolonging it as long as I could. Bash would have to force me to cut the cord soon.

"You're leaving?" Ollie asked quietly, his gray eyes a storm of anger and confusion.

"It's complicated, Ollie," I said. "You know I have a responsibility—"

"But I—"

"It's not just about you, Oliver," Sebastian said. "It's about the Lycan. Our people."

I knew what Ollie wanted to say. *I just turned, we're closer than ever, how could you leave me now?* It was unfair, that much I knew, but I had to go. If I could take him with me, I would, but he was better off staying with the Brooklyn Pack under Jackson's care, with Amy.

At least I'd have three months to spend with him. I planned to milk every second of it.

Ollie didn't say anything, he only turned and left the living room, leaving me and Bash alone. He just needed time to cool down. Eventually I'd sit down with him and explain it all. He'd understand.

"Mackenzie." Bash reached for my hand and I turned to face him. "You didn't shift."

I shook my head. "No time, but I'm okay, I swear. As long as you're okay. How did they get you, anyway?" We moved to the sofa and sat down, making ourselves comfortable.

"I was walking from the house to the Compound. I was almost there, and luckily some of the wolves were looking out the window and saw it happen. Damn warlocks, I didn't even see them," he snarled, running a hand through his hair. He was angry with himself for getting taken.

"It could have happened to anyone," I said. "Especially when they travel in groups. No one could have stood a chance against them."

He stayed silent and I knew it was still bothering him. His ego was bruised. I sighed. *Men.*

I looked toward the stairs and made sure no one was there before scooting closer to Bash. "Listen," I whispered, "there's something I have to tell you. I've sorta been keeping quiet about it, but I think I need to let someone know." I'd mentioned Úlfur to Alexander, but after our initial meeting, I never said anything else about him.

"What is it?" he whispered back with a frown.

"Do you recognize the name Úlfur?"

"No, I don't," Bash said. "Who is he?"

"I don't know." I proceeded to tell him all about the mystery man, starting with our first meeting when Bobby Wu took me to his apartment, until tonight when he threatened me just outside the Compound. I described his physical appearance, his weird British-like accent, and how he always seemed to be smirking like he was in on some joke I wasn't aware of. "I'm not afraid of much, Bash, but I really think this guy can kill me easily. He's dangerous."

"Why didn't you tell me sooner?" he asked, annoyed.

"Because I'm an idiot." I shrugged, not knowing what else to say. "I don't know what he is, but his powers are otherworldly. He's superfast and extra strong. It's like nothing I've ever seen before."

Bash furrowed his brows and rubbed at his chin in thought. "You said he has a British accent?"

"It's weird – like it is, but it's not. I don't know how to explain it."

"Well, his name is definitely *not* British." Bash reached for his phone on the coffee table. He started fiddling with it and I peered over his shoulder to see what he was up to.

"What are you doing?" I asked.

"Googling the origin of his name," he said. "If I can get the spelling right."

"What does it say?"

Bash tensed and those ocean blue eyes snapped in my direction. Trouble was written all over his expression. I knew that whatever he was about to say, I wouldn't like it.

"Úlfur is Icelandic. And it means wolf."

ABOUT THE AUTHOR

Join my Facebook group, **Karina's Kick-Ass Reads** to learn more about future projects, as well as stay up to date with the next book in the Mackenzie Grey series.

Reviews are very important to authors and help readers discover our books. Please take a moment to leave a review. Thank you!

ALSO BY KARINA ESPINOSA

Mackenzie Grey: Origins Series (Completed)

SHIFT

CAGED

ALPHA

OMEGA

Mackenzie Grey: Trials Series

From the Grave

Curse Breaker

Bound by Magic

The Last Valkyrie Series (Completed)

The Last Valkyrie

The Sword of Souls

The Rise of the Valkyries

ABOUT THE AUTHOR

Karina Espinosa is the Urban Fantasy Author of the Mackenzie Grey novels and The Last Valkyrie series. An avid reader throughout her life, the world of Urban Fantasy easily became an obsession that turned into a passion for writing strong leading characters with authentic story arcs. When she isn't writing badass heroines, you can find this self-proclaimed nomad in her South Florida home binge watching the latest series on Netflix or traveling far and wide for the latest inspiration for her books.

For more information:
www.karinaespinosa.com